I0622209

PURE

VENGEANCE

Jana Nolan

PURE VENGEANCE

Jana Nolan

Earth Star Publications
www.earthstarpublications.com

FIRST EDITION
First Printing May 2016

ISBN 978-0-944851-44-9

Printed in the United States of America

INTRODUCTION

For those of you who aren't familiar with, or have read, any of my books, I would like to say that this book was a real challenge for me to write.

Certain parts of the stories were told to me by family members with a fictional imagination such as myself. I took some of their short stories and made them my own, to create an even larger, more exciting story for you to read.

I grew up in a small town named Montrose, Colorado. Being a country girl, most of my books and stories have revolved around country living or a small town atmosphere.

The title, *PURE VENGEANCE,* was chosen by me because of the fear, and different situations or circumstances that some people have faced or encountered during their lifetimes.

The stories contained in this book will not only thrill you and chill you, they will also make you wonder and think about what could happen in everyday life.

I will be taking you in a whole new direction that you wouldn't think about, or would ever imagine happening to you.

Sit back and enjoy the stories that will give your thoughts a ride of a lifetime.

After reading this book, and all the stories, remember that this book is fiction, and that the stories are just for entertainment ... or are they?

The first story, *"The Old House at the Top of the Hill,"* is a story about a family that moves to a new state to make a good life for themselves. Instead, they find something waiting for them in the old house that they weren't expecting.

The second story, "*The Woman That Wouldn't Let Go*," is about a family that was having a normal every-day life until the past of a person surfaces.

The third story, "*Spring Break*," is about a man who was trying to promote something that was his life's ambition, when he found the woman who changed his way of thinking, and others who wanted to end his life.

The fourth story, "*The Cabin at the End of the Road*," is about a woman who just wanted to enjoy life for the first time in years. The decisions that she made brought havoc to her, and her friends.

Now that I have given you a quick summary of what you will be reading about, it is up to you to decide whether any of these tales are capable of happening at any given moment, or if they are just something that an author/writer such as myself completely made up to captivate her readers.

However you interpret the book, remember that there are strange happenings every day that surround us. With all of this in mind, enjoy the fictional stories that will make you think.

CONTENTS

PART 1
The Old House at the Top of the Hill

PART 2
The Woman That Wouldn't Let Go

PART 3
Spring Break

PART 4
The Cabin at the End of the Road

The Old House at the Top of the Hill

— 1 —

Was Our Journey Worth It?

It's mid June, and the leaves are just now starting to form on the huge trees that surround the entire area. They are bright green in color, and beautiful to look at.

The area that I am referring to is the North Woods of Wisconsin. The winter months are brutal and long. For many people who move here, the weather is more than they can handle.

Some find it hard to survive. Each year the population changes rapidly. When others are moving here to the North Woods to start a life with their family, there are just as many people moving away.

My name is Keli Porter. For a short time, I lived here in the small town of Woodberry, Wisconsin. The town itself is off the beaten path of the larger cities. At the time, my family and I believed it to be the perfect place to live.

In order to tell you my story, I need to go back to many years ago.

Like the ones who moved here with great expectations of a good life for their family, my parents were at the top of the list.

I am the oldest of four children, which includes my two brothers and a baby sister. The reason why we moved to Woodberry was because of an inheritance that was given to our father.

Because of this, my father became the new owner of an old house that happened to be the only one standing at the top of a hill. His Uncle Henry passed away unexpectedly, and in the will he had named my father the beneficiary of it.

There were many looks from the townspeople who lived here when the moving truck pulled up in front of the old house. I was quick to notice that the people standing below the hill were pointing at us and whispering to each other.

Father was helping the driver with hand directions as he backed the huge truck up to the front door of the house. While doing this, Father didn't notice the many people below the hill, watching and talking quietly amongst themselves.

Mother was busy unloading our van and taking what we had brought with us into the house. She was placing the items neatly in a pile in the living room, out of the way of the movers, who also were carrying into the house many boxes and furniture.

Being the oldest child, I was put in charge of my younger brothers and my baby sister, to make sure that they didn't wander off somewhere into the midst of the forest, which partially surrounded the old house. For a very young girl of 10, this was not an easy task.

Even as young as I was, I couldn't help wondering why all of those people continued to feel the need to stand around, watching and talking about us. Later, when the truck was unloaded, there was nothing for the people to see, so they left.

When Mother had time to talk, I asked her why

these people were watching, talking and pointing at us.

Mother replied, "This is a small town, dear. We are new to the area, and they probably were just curious about what we looked like. I am sure that they will come back and introduce themselves to us after they feel that we have had an ample amount of time to get our things organized and situated in this house."

This, at the time, sounded good to me, and so I accepted the words that my mother spoke. Both my father and my mother always seemed to have a way of explaining things to help me understand.

Days went by, and no one came to visit us. Even when we went into town, people stared at us as if we had something dripping from our noses. I then could see that Mother and Father were noticing how we were being treated as well.

Coming from a good family, we were all raised to be respectful to everyone, no matter how they treated us. We smiled and returned to the old house.

The people in town weren't the only things creepy in Woodberry. There were times when I thought that one of my brothers or my sister was talking to me. When I turned around to respond back, there was no one standing there.

I tried shrugging this off as I did know that my imagination had a tendency to be on overload and way out of control. On the other hand, this had happened to me more than once.

This was something that I felt needed to be addressed with my mother and father, but because of feeling weird from the moving-in day here, and somewhat paranoid from the first day, I chose to keep this stuff to myself for now. Maybe it would pass.

How little did I know that before long, my family would also experience unknown happenings in the old house. Sometimes, for me, it was easier to walk out the back door, and walk around in the woods for a while, to clear the thoughts in my head.

When night time came, it was even scarier as my bedroom lights were flickering on and off. At times, my radio would turn itself on and off as well.

My little sister, Ruthie, would come into my bedroom, running at full speed to jump in bed with me. She was only 4, and would only say, "Keli, I am afraid of the boogie man."

I would then try to explain to her that there was no boogie man in the house to be afraid of. This being said, it was hard for me to be convincing as I, too, was afraid of the old house as well.

One day, when Mother and Father put me in charge of watching my siblings, I was downstairs in the living room, trying to turn on the television. My reasoning for doing this at the time was that if Donnie, Jonathan and Ruthie were preoccupied watching a cartoon, it would give me the opportunity to concentrate on homework from school that I needed to get done.

No matter how much effort I put into turning the television on, I had no success at it. Then, when I walked away from it, the television would come on by itself. As I would walk over to it, to change the channel, it would turn itself off. How is this possible?

When Mother and Father walked back through the front door, I was ecstatic to see them. Something was most definitely weird in there, and not normal. Again, I wanted to talk to both Mother and Father about everything I had witnessed when they were home, and just now, when they were gone.

But again, I attributed it to maybe the television starting to break down.

In turn, I went back upstairs to my bedroom to

finish my homework and also to get ready for another day to come, living in that old scary house on the hill.

It was also Picture Day at my school the next day, and I really wanted to look my best. Being showered, having P.J.s on and tiny rollers in my hair, I was ready for bed. Because of the weird and unusual day that I'd had, I was exceptionally tired and fell fast asleep.

The next morning, I was up and running. I had picked out the prettiest dress I had in my closet. Because I had gone to school in a different state, I had a bunch of friends that I wanted to exchange school pictures with. My expectations were for the pictures to be the best ever this year. At least I was leaning in that direction.

I wasn't the only one who had gone all out for Picture Day. My brother Donnie, who was a couple of years younger than I was, had also taken extra time to get ready for school. He had splashed on a tiny bit of my father's cologne and was standing in front of me, combing his hair at what appeared to me to be a thousand times, before he grabbed his school books and started for the front door.

Donnie, being the oldest of my two brothers, was always expected to set a good example for our youngest brother, Jonathan.

On the other hand, our baby sister, Ruthie, whom I was the one expected to set a good example for, was the one that we all tried to watch, to see what she would come up with, or do next.

One time, she would be standing right beside us, as she was told to do, and then when we would turn around to talk to her, she would be nowhere in sight.

I wondered sometimes if she, too, heard someone speaking and went to find out where their voice was coming from, or whom it was coming from.

This time, though, after Donnie shut the door behind himself and Jonathan, I tried turning the knob on the door handle. It wouldn't turn. That was very strange as it had just worked for them. I backed away, staring at it. Then I walked forward, to try to turn the knob again.

This time, it was so hot that I could barely touch it. Backing off once again, Donnie had noticed that I was not with them and came back to find me. When he turned the knob, the door opened for him. He said, "Keli, what is taking you so long? We need to catch the school bus."

In amazement of what had just taken place, I never said a word to Donnie about what had happened to me, except, "Wasn't the door knob burning hot when you opened the door?"

"No, Keli. What is wrong with you? Hurry up! We are going to be late!"

— 2 —
Who and Why?

It seemed like every day at school I was being watched, not only by the other kids, but also by the teachers and staff members. I felt like there was something that they wanted to tell me, but instead chose not to, for some reason.

I had made a couple of new friends who didn't make me feel this way. They were new to the area as well, and probably were as nervous as I was, with just wanting to be accepted by everyone there.

My new friends were Tammy and Tanya. They were twins, and at first I had a hard time telling them apart. Then, one day I noticed a mole on Tanya's neck, and from then on I knew the difference. Funny how that works! They didn't care if they got certain looks from the other students and teachers. This made it easy for us to be friends, as I, too, was starting to get pretty annoyed with, once again, questions that stemmed from when we first arrived in Woodberry.

What was it that made my family and I stand out, to the point of staring and talking behind our backs? The questions in my mind made me wonder if my father's uncle, for no explainable reason, was somewhat a threat to the town, or perhaps something worse.

However, it was that time to stand before the

camera and do the best I could to get a decent picture this year to hand out to Tammy, Tanya and my friends back in Illinois, where I had just come from.

Tammy and Tanya wanted to come home with me after school, but had gotten news that this would need to take place another day. So I left and went to look for Donnie and Jonathan, to make sure that they were standing at the spot where the bus would pick us up at school to take us home.

Donnie had made some new friends. Jonathan just wanted to tag along and make sure that he was also included in everything that Donnie and his friends did. This worked for a little while, and then it was time for Jonathan to go find someone his own age to play with.

Things had circulated in the old house that were bothering my mother and father. They, too, experienced something that I would find out about later on. They both chose to wait to talk to me about it, as they were also making excuses for the mystery of what was going on in the old house that day.

During school, Mother had gone to the kitchen sink to do the breakfast dishes. My father had gone outside to fire up his chainsaw, so that he could go behind the old house to cut down some old trees for firewood to place in the wood stove. That big old house was very drafty and the wood stove would help keep us warmer.

As Mother was washing dishes, she thought she heard someone talking in the living room. She was convinced that some of the people in the town had come there to visit and get to know us.

She put the dish rag down in the sink and took off the rubber gloves that she was wearing. There was a rack underneath the sink, where she always placed them, to help them to dry out until she needed to use them again. So she neatly hung the gloves there.

When Mother walked into the living room, there was no one in the room but herself. She then stood in the living room, wondering who it could have been that she was hearing, and why they had left so fast.

After much contemplation, she returned to the kitchen sink to complete her job of washing the dishes. The rubber gloves that she had neatly placed on the rack underneath the sink were sitting on the counter next to it.

This was something that sent her outside to talk to my father. "Tom, I had the strangest thing happen to me in the house just now."

"Oh, what was that, Connie"

"I was getting ready to do dishes and I thought that you had come back into the house with neighbors who had come to visit us. I stopped what I was doing at the sink and placed my rubber gloves below the sink on a rack that I have used under the sink in every house we have lived in. I place them there to dry out, until I use them again. Then, I went into the living room to be with you and our new neighbors.

"When I got in there, no one was there! I even looked out the front door, to check and see if maybe you had gone outside with them. Nobody was there. I stood there questioning what I had heard in the living room, and then returned to the kitchen to finish the dishes. Sitting next to the sink were the rubber gloves that I distinctly remember placing on the rack below to dry, before I left to go to the other room."

"Connie, are you sure that you were completely focused on this? And just maybe *thought* you had put your gloves there?"

"Yes, Tom. I mean, I might have imagined hearing

people talking in the living room, but I have always placed the gloves below my kitchen sink to dry when I wasn't wearing them."

"Maybe through anticipation of new neighbors coming to visit, you thought you did that this time."

"Maybe, Tom," Mother replied as she turned to walk back into the house, imagining what she *maybe* had done and being as confused as ever.

My father had just come from the back porch, where he kept his chainsaw and other tools that he had chosen to bring with us. Before leaving the back porch, Father unplugged the extension cord from the plug-in. He picked up his saw and had forgotten to grab his sharpener. When he noticed this, he returned to the back porch to grab it. As he turned around to walk away, he noticed the extension cord plugged back into the electrical socket on the wall.

Father was very careful to unplug or disconnect electrical apparatus before working on anything that could or would shock or electrocute him. So, like Mother walking back to the house, wondering what was wrong with her, Father was also thinking how strange and bizarre that occurrence was as well.

Father could see Mother standing at the kitchen sink and also knew that she couldn't have gotten to the back porch without him seeing her. He knew she would never plug in anything that he was using, if she saw it unplugged.

After Father had sharpened the saw, he resumed his day of cutting firewood for us. It was supposed to be even colder this year in the North Woods of Wisconsin.

As Father returned to the house and the kitchen, he was talking to Mother as he poured them both a cup of coffee. "Connie, you aren't the only one who is questioning actions today. I had to go back to the porch to get the chainsaw sharpener today, after I went outside to cut some trees for firewood. When I went back there, I saw that the extension cord was plugged back into the electrical socket. You know how I am about checking and rechecking my movements before I start any kind of a project. This was so strange and bizarre. It isn't like me to forget to unplug something," Father said.

"I know, Tom. It looks like we both lost our minds today, temporarily." Mother laughed.

"I'm not sure what happened, Connie. I have been thinking about this all day and had a hard time focusing on what I was doing. I don't think it would be a good idea to mention any of this to the kids. We don't want to scare them in any way."

"I agree, Tom. The kids are trying to adjust to living in a new house just like we are. If we feel later that we need to tell them about this, we will."

That night as we sat there having supper, I noticed that Mother and Father were quieter than usual. This was not like either one of them to at least ask us how our day at school had been. Father was picking at his food and suddenly put his napkin on his plate. He had eaten hardly anything and was getting up to pour himself another cup of coffee. I could see that he was strongly thinking about something.

Mother noticed it too, but kept quiet. Donnie also saw that Father was worrying, or thinking about something, but still asked him if—after they were done eating—he would go outside with them and toss the ball around for a while. Father told him that it was too cold, and they would do it another time.

Before, neither the weather nor the temperature outside had ever stopped Father from wanting to play ball with his kids. Instead, we were told that after we finished eating supper, we should probably go upstairs and get started early on our homework.

Donnie looked at me as if he was wondering why Father was in such deep thought.

There was something pretty heavy weighing on Father's mind, and at the moment, we had no idea what it was.

— 3 —

Unsettled

As I lay in bed that night, I could hear Father pacing around the living room and the kitchen. I knew that he was in deep thought about something.

I knew that Mother had already gone to bed as I had heard her climbing the old crackly stairs earlier. As for Father, there was something that he needed to work through in his mind. What I didn't know was that Father was reliving his actions from earlier today, trying to figure out how and why Mother and himself had unknown experiences that day that definitely were unusual and unexplainable.

I stayed awake as long as I could, waiting for Father to go to bed, but eventually fell fast asleep.

When morning came, Donnie, Jonathan, Ruthie and I were up and ready for what we hoped to be a fun-filled day. It was the weekend and there was no school.

As I entered the kitchen, I saw Mother sitting at the kitchen table, deep in thought. She had her head in her hands and was staring at the table.

"Mother, is there something wrong?"

"Nothing for you to worry about, Keli. I guess I am just a little tired today," Mother said to me.

"I'm sorry, Mama. I heard Father walking around down here very late last night, until I couldn't stay awake any longer. When we were eating dinner, Donnie and I noticed that you and Father were very quiet. Is there anything that you would like to talk to me about?"

"Not right now, Keli. Yes, Father was up late last night. He was trying to work out some things in his mind. Nothing for you to be concerned with. Father and I have talked about it and are sure that it is nothing."

I had listened to Mother's words, but even though I was only 10 years old, I could see that even Mother was pondering something over, trying to find answers to whatever it was that was preying heavily on her mind.

Mother got up from the table and said, "Keli, go find Donnie, Jonathan and Ruthie. I want all of you to come down here so that your father can sleep. It was early this morning before he finally came to bed. I will fix all of you breakfast, and then I want all of you to go outside and play," Mother said.

"Okay, Mama."

In my way of thinking, I was wondering if Mama wanted us outside so that when Father did come downstairs, they could talk privately.

I went back upstairs to their bedroom, to tell them what Mother had said. I told them that we were going to be extra quiet, so Father could sleep, and after breakfast we were going outside to play for the remainder of the day, or until we got told to come back inside the old house.

Later that morning, as Donnie and Jonathan were tossing a baseball back and forth to one another, I was sitting on the ground with Ruthie, looking through the grass, to see if we could find a four-leaf clover to take to Mother.

I happened to look up and into the kitchen

window. I noticed Father and Mother sitting at the kitchen table, talking. My curiosity of wondering why Mother and Father looked so sad and distracted was wanting to get the best of me. I thought about entering the house to listen quietly to the conversation, so that maybe with knowing what was happening to them, I might be able to help.

Instead, I stayed with Ruthie on the grass.

This is one of many conversations of Mother's and Father's that I had missed:

"Tom, both of us had an off day yesterday. We have been living here now for a week, and what happened to both of us was just our forgetfulness. Nothing more."

"I did a lot of thinking, and pacing the floor last night down here, trying to make sense out of what happened to us yesterday," said Father. "At first, I thought that your desire to have company might have misled your mind into believing that you heard someone talking in the living room, but when I went back to get my chainsaw sharpener and discovered what I did, I couldn't get it out of my mind. If I didn't know better, I would think that someone or something was trying to make us both go crazy."

"I'm sorry, Tom. It kept me awake last night for quite a while as well, going over in my mind my actions. I can see why you had a hard time sleeping. I did discover one thing, though. I didn't like being in this old house with you not lying next to me in bed."

"I'm sorry too, Connie. I'm sure that we just had an off day. Let's try to get this out of our minds and go on with our day," Father said.

I was still watching from the back yard and saw Father hug Mother. At this time, I thought that maybe they'd had just a small argument and that was the reason for Father's pacing last night and Mother's sadness this morning. It looked like they had made up.

It wasn't long before Father came outside and started tossing the ball to Donnie and Jonathan. Mother was in the house alone and feeling a very cold chill. The air had changed from being too warm to feeling like she was standing in a closed freezer.

As she walked out of the kitchen and into Father's study, a book fell off the shelf. It hit the floor, which startled Mother. She bent down and picked it up. Placing it back on the shelf, where she believed the book had been, she turned around to walk away.

Again, she heard the book hit the floor. Instead of picking it back up again, she left it alone on the floor. Mother also chose not to mention any of this to Father. It would mean another sleepless night for him.

In her mind, she was wondering if Woodberry had small earthquakes from time to time. The North Woods of Wisconsin was full of all kinds of surprises. Maybe a tremor had caused the book to fall.

The chill in the air had gone away as fast as it appeared. Mother started blaming her chill on the fact that she must be going through the change of life. She wanted Father in bed with her sleeping that night, and not up pacing the downstairs again.

Shortly after this, Father brought us back into the house for a cup of hot chocolate. The weather was very frigid and had changed for the day.

After finishing the hot chocolate, Donnie, Jonathan, Ruthie and myself returned to our bedrooms. I was working on a project for school. Donnie and Jonathan were playing with toy cars, and Ruthie was in her room, playing with her doll house.

After a while, I went to check on her, to help Mother and Father keep an eye on her. Before I opened her bedroom door, I could hear her talking to someone.

"Why did you think I wouldn't return?" Ruthie said.

I opened her door and saw that no one besides her was in the room. I asked Ruthie, "Who are you talking to?"

"Keli, I have a new friend. She is playing dolls with me. Her name is Sally. Do you want to sit down on the floor and play with us too?" Ruthie asked.

"No, Ruthie, not at this time. I need to go downstairs and talk to Mama and Father," I frantically replied back.

"Okay, Keli," Ruthie said.

When I left the room and shut her door, I heard her say, "It's okay. Keli is my big sister. You can trust her."

With this being said, I ran down the upstairs hallway and down the crackly stairs to the kitchen, where Mother and Father were sitting at the table, talking again.

"Mother, Father ... something is wrong with Ruthie!" I practically yelled out.

"What, Keli, is wrong?" Father jumped to his feet, ready to run up to Ruthie's room.

"I heard her talking to someone in her room when I went to check on her, to make sure she didn't go back outside alone. When I opened her bedroom door, she told me that she had a new friend by the name of Sally. She asked me if I wanted to sit down on the floor and play with them. I told her no, and that I needed to talk to both of you."

"Don't be alarmed, Keli. It isn't anything unusual for a young child to have an imaginary friend to play with. I'm sure that she gets lonely when she has no one to play with, and so she made up one to keep her company," Mother replied back.

"Okay, Mama. I didn't know this, but do now. I won't worry anymore."

Little did we know that this was still going to continue to go on in Ruthie's bedroom, and that it *was* something to worry about.

Upstairs, Ruthie said, "Yes, I will do whatever you want me to do. I trust you."

— 4 —
Watchful Eye

The rest of the day seemed to go fairly well. The book that had fallen off the shelf was in place on the book shelf when Mother went to put it back. Seeing it in place, she then believed that Father had seen it lying on the floor and had picked it up to return it to its place on the shelf, where it belonged.

Again she felt a shivering chill in the room and put more wood in the wood stove. As she was leaving the room, she glanced at the thermostat. It was registering 90 degrees, but yet once again, the room felt like it was at minus-25. This felt strange to her, as Father had just bought the thermostat new from the hardware store when they went to town.

Not wanting to bother Father again with this, Mother turned out the light, then walked up the crackly stairs to make her way to her and Father's bedroom. Tonight she hoped that Father and herself would sleep calmer and more peacefully than they had slept the night before.

Around midnight, when everyone was sleeping, Father woke up to use the bathroom. When he entered the room, he noticed a strange metallic smell. His arms were breaking out into chills. At that moment, he had a strange feeling of malice in the room. It was as if a malevolent gaze were fixed upon him.

Father felt as if he was being watched, and it gave him the creeps. The only one in the bedroom besides himself was Mother, and she was sound asleep. Father turned the light out in the bathroom, and not wanting to awaken Mother with this, sat down in a lounge chair close to the bed.

The feeling of being watched didn't go away. He felt that his night of sleeping had ended. With more questions that needed to be answered, like the ones from the night before, he paced all over the downstairs. Father was consumed with many thoughts.

Whereas in Ruthie's room, at the end of the upstairs hallway, Ruthie was sitting on the floor with her doll house, talking again to an unseen person that wasn't going away in Ruthie's mind.

"I am so happy I have a new friend that lives in this house with me and my family. I want to stay here with you forever."

There was a hesitation as if Ruthie was being replied to, and then she replied back to this invisible friend with excitement in her voice, "Whatever you tell me to do, I will do."

Unfortunately, Ruthie's room and Mother's and Father's room were far enough apart where Father couldn't hear her speaking.

The talking between Ruthie and the invisible friend continued most of the night as Father sat in the chair, still feeling like there was someone or something watching him.

When morning daylight came, Mother woke up to the sound of Father downstairs in the kitchen. Mother slipped on her slippers and bathrobe, to join him in the kitchen. By the time she walked down the old rickety staircase with the crackly stairs, Father had heard her coming and poured her a hot cup of coffee.

"Good morning, Tom. How long have you been awake?"

"Good morning, Connie. I have been awake since around midnight."

"Why? What happened?" Mother asked.

"When I got up to use the bathroom last night, it felt like I was being watched by someone or something," Father told her. "All of this gave me the creeps. I could see that it wasn't you. Not wanting to wake you up, I sat in the chair the rest of the night. You were sleeping very sound. In the bathroom there was a strong metallic smell. My arms were covered with goose bumps, which gave me the creeps. I am convinced that there is something in this old house, Connie. So many things are pointing toward this."

Then Mother told him, "I didn't want to mention this to you, as after what we both experienced the other day, I wanted you and me to get a good night's rest, and I knew that if I told you any of what had happened next with me, you would be wondering and thinking about it all night.

"Now that this has happened, I will share with you what happened with *me* yesterday. When I went into your study again, to place a book that had fallen from the shelf while I was in there, that scared me when it fell, I bent down and picked it up to return it to the place where I believed it had fallen from on the book shelf. After I put it back, when I turned my back to walk away, it fell once again. So I left it on the floor. Tom, do they have earthquakes or tremors here in Wisconsin in the North Woods?"

"Not that I am aware of," Father replied.

"Okay, then did you find the book on the floor and return it to the book shelf?"

"No, but maybe Keli saw it there and put it back, and just didn't say anything to either one of us about it," said Father.

"Also, Tom, I think you need to take back the new thermostat that you just bought. At that time as well, when I was in your study, the air turned bitter cold. It felt like I was standing inside a closed freezer. To me, it was time to put more wood in the wood stove. As I was leaving the study, I looked at the thermostat. It registered 90 degrees. It has to be broken."

"Later today," said Father, "I will go to town and exchange it, or get a better one. Sometimes they aren't accurate, and this might be the case with this one."

By the time Father had finished talking, Donnie, Jonathan, Ruthie and I had entered the room.

Mother was fixing breakfast and asked us, after we had eaten, if we wanted to go into town with her and Father. Of course we said yes.

— 5 —

Truth Be Known

Driving into town, Father pointed out many things that he recalled from his childhood in the North Woods. It was not only beautiful there, but Father told us that next summer he would take us to the Great Lakes, not far from the North Woods..

When we reached Woodberry, there—standing on the corner, staring at us—were other people than the ones who had been standing at the bottom of the hill watching us when we had moved in.

Mother, of course, stood up for them. "This really isn't unusual behavior. We are new here with Illinois license plates. They might have noticed this and are commenting amongst themselves about it."

Whatever their excuse was, I'm not sure that Father accepted any of the townspeople's behavior. He didn't say anything, but the look on his face said a lot.

As we pulled up to the hardware store, Father parked our car. As he was climbing out, he told us to stay in it. He would only be a few minutes. He grabbed the bag with the thermostat and assured Mother that the next one would work.

After entering the store, he saw the store manager standing close to the entrance. "Excuse me, sir. I need to return this item and exchange it for something better."

"Sure, what is it that you are returning?" the store manager asked.

"A thermostat that I bought here the other day. It appears to not be working properly."

"Okay, follow me, and we will get you all fixed up. By the way, you look a lot like a man that used to live in this area. He is no longer with us. By chance, are you related to Henry Porter?"

"Yes, he was my Uncle Henry before he passed away."

"Okay, I see the resemblance even more now. That was a shame what happened to him. I guess when his wife and kids left him all alone, it was more than he could handle."

Father said to him, "When I found out that I was his sole relative and had inherited the old house on the hill, I wasn't told any details about his death. In fact, I didn't even know he was married and had kids," added Father.

"Yes, he had a daughter and a son. His daughter was 6, and I believe his son was 7. His wife was a nice-looking woman who appeared to be much younger than he was. There was talk around town that she had been messing around on Henry with a younger man. I also heard that they fought a lot, and that Henry liked to drink. He would, at times, hang out at the bar until it closed for the night. Then, when he returned home to find her waiting up for him, a huge fight would start. And from what I heard, he would hit her and knock her to the floor. I guess when he was at the bar, he would hear stories of her seeing another man, and this would cause Henry to leave the bar in a rage. Then, of course, this is just what I heard. I probably shouldn't have told you all, or any, of this."

"That's quite all right. This explains the looks

that we have been getting from people since we arrived here. Especially where I look so much like Uncle Henry. The one thing I would like to know next is how Uncle Henry passed away. I was just told that he had an unusual death, unexpectedly."

"Yes, this is true. He was found hanging from a big tree with a rope tied around his neck. The people who found him said that he had a horrified expression on his face. Some people in town that knew him believe that he went crazy and that he was the one who killed himself."

"Thank you for telling me all of this," said Father. "Since we have been here, we haven't had one neighbor call on us. My family and I were wondering why, and now I think I know."

Father shook the man's hand and thanked him again for all his help. After exchanging the thermostat, he returned to the car.

"Connie, I met a nice man in the store who explained a lot to me. When we return home, I will tell you what he said."

"Okay, Tom," Mother replied.

In other words, none of what Father wanted to tell Mother was anything that Father thought we should hear.

— 6 —

Unseen Saga

After we arrived home, us kids were instructed by Father to play outside for a while, as he wanted to speak with Mother alone.

When they entered the house, the discussion began.

"Connie, I know now why everyone in town is looking at us and watching us the way that they are."

"I'm glad, but how do you know?" Mother asked.

"The manager of the hardware store noticed that I look a lot like Uncle Henry. He told me things that I didn't know about until today. Me being the only one left in his immediate family, other than a wife and kids that I didn't know about, I have no way of contacting anyone to check the man at the hardware's story out, to see if all of this that I just heard is true.

"My gut feeling tells me that this man isn't just making up anything of what he told me. It appears that Uncle Henry liked to drink. His wife was quite a bit younger than he was. They had two kids together. The man said he believed their daughter was 6 and their son was 7.

"When Uncle Henry went to the bar, he would hear stories of how his wife was messing around with a younger man than himself. This news would drive

Uncle Henry crazy with jealousy, and he would fester on it and think about everything that he had heard that night in the bar.

"After he returned here, he would beat up his wife. The townspeople stopped seeing her in town, and the kids quit going to school here. The story is that she got sick of him and of getting beat up, and took the kids and left town, never to be seen again. The story is that after a point, either out of loneliness or going insane, they found his body dangling from a tree in the back yard, with a rope tied around his neck. No one suspected foul play. I guess the look on his face was that of fear.

"Like the man in the hardware store said, he believes that could be the reason why we are getting looks, is because I look so much like Uncle Henry that it is a little strange for the people here. Especially for those people who knew him. So, knowing this, the whispers and looks might not really have much to do with *us*, as the townspeople might be remembering Uncle Henry, his life, and his death that he scheduled for himself."

"Wow, Tom! This is quite the story," said Mother. "You picked the right person to talk to today!"

"Now, with this being said, it still leaves me with unanswered questions on why we have experienced what we have in this old house," Father answered.

"I agree with you, and I'm not sure if we should talk to any of the kids about this," Mother said.

"All we can do is wait to see if things continue to happen. Then, if we need to, we will make a decision on what we need to do next."

Mother once again agreed with Father. After their discussion, Father told us that we could return to the house again if we were ready to come inside to play.

Father installed the new thermostat and Donnie

and Jonathan carried their toy electric train set downstairs.

Mother returned to her daily duties of house cleaning. Being somewhat afraid to go upstairs by herself, she went anyway. She wanted to get over her fear of the old house.

Ruthie didn't have any kind of fear of it, as she had already returned to her bedroom and her doll house. Mother was going from bedroom to bedroom, gathering dirty clothes from all the hampers. When she reached Ruthie's room, she—like me—heard Ruthie talking to an unseen person.

What Mother heard was out of the ordinary. She barely opened Ruthie's door so that she could quietly listen to what Ruthie was saying.

"How long will it take? Yes, I want to be with you." There was a slight hesitation after Ruthie spoke, as if she could hear her friend talking back to her. Then Ruthie said, "Where will my Mama, Father, Keli, Donnie and Jonathan go?"

By then, Mother had heard enough. She felt a chill in the air just as she had felt in herself downstairs, and she could smell a horrible odor. "Ruthie!"

"Oh hello, Mama. I was just talking to my new friend, Sally. Isn't she pretty, Mama?"

"Ruthie, I think you are spending too much time in your room and should go downstairs now to be with your father, brothers and sister," Mother said firmly.

"But, Mama, I like staying in my room and playing and talking to Sally."

"Don't argue with me, Ruthie! Just do as I tell you to do."

"Okay, Mama. I will see you later, Sally." As Ruthie left the room, she slammed the door behind her.

Mother bent down to pick up the doll house and

put it back on the shelf with more of Ruthie's toys. When she grabbed for the doll house, Mother could feel extreme heat coming from it. She stopped and left it alone.

Sally, the unseen friend of Ruthie's, had expressed her anger because Ruthie had listened to Mother, not her, and had gone downstairs.

Mother backed up to the door and then turned the door handle and left the room. She was on her way down the long, scary hallway upstairs, to talk to Father. When she approached him, she once again told him to meet her in the kitchen.

"Keli, I need you to keep your sister down here with you."

"Okay, Mama," I replied.

Father had gotten up from the floor, where he was sitting as he was playing trains with Donnie and Jonathan. When Father entered the kitchen, he asked, "What is it, Connie, that you need to talk to me about away from the children? Why isn't Ruthie allowed in her room now?"

"I was upstairs going from bedroom to bedroom, gathering all the laundry. When I reached Ruthie's bedroom, I overheard her talking. I quietly opened the door just enough to hear the one-sided conversation that she was having with her invisible friend. When Ruthie would speak, there would be a hesitation as if she could hear another person talking to her. Then she would speak again."

"What was being said?" Father asked.

"Ruthie, not knowing that I was there, said, 'How long will it take?' Then she said, 'Yes, I just want to be with you.' Again after a hesitation, she said, 'Where will Mama, Father, Keli, Donnie and Jonathan go?' I then made Ruthie aware of my presence in her room.

She told me that she was just talking to her new friend, Sally. She also said, 'Isn't she pretty, Mama?' This is when I told her that she is spending too much time in her room and to come downstairs and to stay with all of you.

"Of course, she argued with me as she didn't want to leave. I had to be firm with her, and when she left her room, she slammed her bedroom door. When I bent down to pick up the doll house to return it to the shelf, I could feel extreme heat coming from it. I left it alone on the floor and backed up to the door to leave and come find you, so that we could talk."

"That is strange, all right. Was the doll house close to the heat register?"

"Yes, Tom, but it shouldn't have been so hot that I could feel the heat from it before I touched it," Mother replied.

"Maybe, Connie, the heat from the register was blowing on the plastic doll house long enough to make it appear hotter than it was. Also, Ruthie is not good about putting her toys away, so the plastic doll house may have been there for days and just didn't have time to cool down before the hot air from the register kicked on again."

"Maybe," Mother replied with a confused look on her face.

"It is a cold day today," Father said.

"I know, Tom, but there is more to tell you. When I entered her room, I felt a freezing chill again. I also smelled an odor similar to the one that you smelled the other night."

"Again, Connie, this old house is very drafty, and with it being on a hill, we are bound to feel the cold wind and freezing temperatures through the cracks and windows. I will see what I can do to fix this problem.

As for the odor, I am not sure what it is that is causing this. Remember what you told Keli, that it is normal for a young child to make up an imaginary friend. I wouldn't put too much thought into the words that were coming out of Ruthie's mouth, and yes, I agree about her spending too much time in her room. I will ask Keli if she will play more with her for now, until she can get used to her new home and maybe find a real friend."

"Okay, Tom. You are probably right about all of this. I will try hard to relax and overlook some of the things I have been thinking and worrying about."

Again the conversation had ended, and Mother had picked up her clothes basket to take the clothes to the laundry room.

Father returned to the living room to sit on the floor and play toy trains with Donnie and Jonathan, as Keli put fingernail polish on Ruthie's fingernails.

For the moment, all appeared to be calm in the house.

— 7 —

Questions

For the next few days to come, the unusual activity in the house appeared to be fairly normal. If it wasn't, it was only because Mother or Father chose to overlook it.

Ruthie was back to spending more time in her room than she had been doing. I tried to occupy her with different suggestions on journeys that she and I could take so that we could spend more time together. Nothing I mentioned to her interested her. She was in her bedroom most of the time, and in her own world.

I noticed her skin color was becoming very pale. Not to mention the red circles that were forming around her eyes. She was quieter than usual around all of us, and Mother and Father attributed her paleness to being caused from lack of sunshine, as for many months in the North Woods, there is very little of this.

The weather had changed to bitter cold and every day when the weekend came and there was no school, we weren't allowed to go outside unless it was an emergency of some sort.

The manager that Father met at the hardware store, by the name of Dan Roberts, had become pretty good friends with Father. He brought his wife and children over to meet us, and then he would come over to visit with Father by himself at times.

Every time they all came, Dan's daughter would want to play with Ruthie. This would be perfect as then Ruthie would actually have a playmate that all of us could see. Unfortunately, tonight—like every other time Dan and all of his family came over—Ruthie told Mother and Father that she was sick and just wanted to stay in her room and sleep.

Tonight I waited for the perfect time, and then quietly went up the stairs to Ruthie's room. She was laughing and talking again to this invisible friend that had her so preoccupied, she didn't even want to come down and eat, go to school, or spend time with her family.

One of the questions that came up that night was if any of Dan's children had gone to school with Uncle Henry's two children. Dan's wife told Mother that yes, her daughter knew both of the kids. She said that her daughter referred to the little girl as Sally.

Mother sat in the kitchen in amazement, as that was Ruthie's invisible friend's name.

Once again, Mother's wheels were turning in her head, trying to figure out if this was just a coincidence, or if there was more to Ruthie and her new, unseen friend.

Father and Dan spent their time in the study, as Father showed him some hunting trophies that he had. It wasn't long after that when Father and Dan came out of the room and announced that they were going bowling together in a couple of weeks.

Mother, I could see, was not wanting this to happen, as she still feared being left alone for any length of time in the old scary house. She was afraid of what she could witness while Father was gone, yet she didn't want to discourage him from having a friend, or having some fun without us.

By the time Dan and his family left, it was time for all of us to go to bed.

The next morning, Mother, as she did her morning cleaning, returned to Father's study. As she stood there dusting, she noticed that the books were taken out of their categories and put in alphabetical order. This had changed, as Father and herself always put their favorite books—and the children's books—in the book shelf in different spots, and had never had any of them in alphabetical order. Thinking back on the book that kept falling from the shelf, she went to my room to ask questions.

"Keli, this might seem like a strange question to you, but I need to ask you anyway."

"It's okay, Mama. What do you want to ask me?"

"A while back, did you put a book that was laying on the floor back in the book shelf in the study?"

"No, Mama," I replied.

Mother, knowing that Donnie, Jonathan and Ruthie weren't tall enough, again had a weird feeling and a strange look on her face.

"Okay, Keli. I just needed to ask."

With my answer, she left the room. After returning downstairs, Mother went back to Father's study to look again. By then, the books had been changed back to the way that Father and herself had them.

Father had gone into town. Keli, Jonathan, Donnie and Ruthie were upstairs. Mother knew then that she wasn't alone in that room, or in the old house. She could feel someone or something watching her.

Could all of this just stem from her being afraid in that old house, and she was imagining things because Father was gone? The book that was on the floor that had fallen had managed to place itself back where it was put when we moved into the house.

Mother wanted to pretend in her mind that all of this was a horrible dream, and that we were still living in our old calm, uneventful house in Illinois. She was frightened.

With a dazed look on her face, she left the study to return to the kitchen and wait for Father to get back from town. When he did return, Mother didn't tell him anything about the books. Instead, she just sat at the table, not saying a word.

"Are you all right, Connie?" Father asked her.

"Yes, I think I just need to sit here and rest for a while."

"Okay. You have been working very hard. Just rest awhile, and then you will feel better," Father replied.

"I hope I can feel better, Tom."

"Today Dan and I talked. We have moved our bowling outing up a week."

Mother said nothing. Father noticed how quiet Mother was, but just attributed it to her being tired. The old house was much bigger than any we had ever lived in, and a lot more work for her to keep clean. Mother continued to sit there at the table and stare with a blank look on her face. Again, she was deep in thought.

Jonathan had brought his toy train set down-stairs again, and Father sat down on the floor to play trains with him. Mother, for hours, sat at the table, pondering over everything in her mind. Ruthie continued to stay in her bedroom. Donnie joined Father and Jonathan in the living room. I came down to sit and work on homework for school.

Other than Mother staring with a blank look, the rest of the day went fairly well. I had stopped visiting

Ruthie's room after being told that she was fine. I could see that things were not right, but being the kid, it was expected of me to follow and do what was told to me.

The next morning, before preparing to go to school, Ruthie once again was refusing Mother, as Mother stood outside her bedroom door, telling her to come downstairs to eat breakfast.

Mother opened her bedroom door and saw her lying in bed. Mother said, "Ruthie, you have five minutes to get down the stairs and sit at the table with us to eat breakfast before you go to preschool today."

Ruthie, refusing, said, "No, Mama, I am not hungry. I just want to stay in my room."

Mother, feeling angry, said, "Ruthie, I am not asking. I am *telling* you to do this. You don't have a say in this. You better be sitting in your chair at the table in five minutes!" Mother's patience with Ruthie was running out since her behavior had changed.

Ruthie, being defiant, met Mother in the upstairs hallway with a scowl on her face. Her arms were crossed and she stomped her feet going down each step in the staircase on her way downstairs to the kitchen. She sat there, picking at her food, and kept saying, "I don't want to eat. I shouldn't have to. Sally doesn't eat and she isn't made to."

Ruthie's change of personality was not only becoming annoying for Mother, but also for Father.

Father said, "Ruthie, you *will* eat. It might take you all day sitting in that chair, but you will not be allowed back upstairs to play with your doll house and your invisible friend, until you have finished every-thing on your plate. Your mother worked hard on this breakfast and you are going to eat it. We are getting tired of your attitude around here, and things are changing as of now. When Dan Porter brings his daughter over to play with you, you will come downstairs and play with her. Also, if things don't change, you won't be allowed to even go back into your bedroom to be by yourself with this new invisible friend of yours."

At that moment, the house shook some. It was again Sally telling Father that she didn't like what he told Ruthie.

Ruthie just looked up at Father with the same scowl that she had given Mother. Father was right. Ruthie had changed. She didn't want to spend time with any of us anymore. She just wanted to stay in her room with her doll house and with her unseen friend.

The color in her face was even more pale now than it had ever been, and the circles around her eyes were even darker in color. When we lived in Illinois, it was very cold there as well, but her color didn't change during the winter like it did here.

Mother kept looking at Ruthie as she, too, had noticed this change in her skin color. There was so much that she needed to talk to Father about, but once again she was afraid that Father would only think that she was so stressed out that she was losing her mind.

After breakfast, Father told Ruthie to go upstairs and get ready for school. He would be driving her to school, whereas Donnie, Jonathan and myself would be taking the bus. Of course, Ruthie mumbled and grumbled all the way up the stairs, and she told Father that she was sick and didn't want to go.

Father again told her that her attitude had better go back to the way that it was before, as Mother and himself had enough of the way that she was behaving.

When Father and Ruthie walked out the door, Mother was alone in that big scary house miles from neighbors or town. She was feeling anxious and felt that the only safe place in the house without Father being there was in her kitchen.

Mother had felt the room shake some and didn't know if Father had, as he was so mad at Ruthie and had been talking to her at the time. Father had said that he would only be a short time being gone. Mother sat at the table, waiting patiently for his return, again wondering why or what was causing her fear of the old house on the hill.

After about an hour, Mother heard what she thought to be footsteps upstairs. Then she thought she heard footsteps coming down the steps with the stairs cracking with what appeared to be each step, from the top of the staircase downward to the living room. Not knowing what to do, or where to run, she sat there, waiting for whatever, or whoever, it was to finally make their appearance known to her.

Instead, she smelled the horrible odor again as she had in Ruthie's room. The only thing she knew to do was to sit there and wait, knowing that she was being watched. Once again, she wasn't going to tell Father as she was starting to believe herself that because of her fear of living in that old scary house, she was losing her mind. She wanted to run out of there as fast as she could.

As Mother got up from the table to leave the house, the front door opened. Father was home. Mother wanted to cry with joy, but held back the tears.

"Connie, I'm home," Father yelled out.

"I know, Tom. I heard you come in the house. How was Ruthie when you got her to school?"

"She complained the whole way there, saying that she didn't want to go. She said she just wanted to be with Sally," Father replied.

"Tom, I thought that her imaginary friend would

go away by now. Have you noticed that her color is very pale, and that she has circles around her eyes that are getting darker each day? She says that she is sick. I am wondering if she actually is and thinking that we need to take her to a doctor to get her checked out.

"Her desire to be with any of us has gone away. She always loved hanging out with Keli, and going on adventures with her. Now she doesn't even want to come downstairs to eat with us, or go to preschool. Tom, she *loved* preschool. She always told me that she was a big girl like Keli. In some way, I feel that this house is affecting her."

"I do, too, Connie. I agree with her seeing a doctor. There is something happening to her. Her being so consumed with an unseen girl frightens me now. She wants to be just like Sally. Whatever this is, I don't like it. I, too, am worried about her and afraid that if we don't get this taken care of now, it could affect the other children or one of us."

"Call a doctor, Tom. We need to get to the bottom of this before things get worse around here."

With Father saying what he did, Mother was ready to tell him everything when the house phone rang. It was the school telling Mother and Father that Ruthie was running a temperature and that one of them needed to come back and get her from school, so she didn't infect the other students in class.

Father told the lady on the phone that they would be there shortly. When Father got off the phone, he had Mother look up the number of the doctor's office in Woodberry.

When he called them, to see if he could bring Ruthie in, Father was told that the doctor was out of town that day and the earliest appointment he could get was the following week. This would have to do.

Instead of just Father going to get Ruthie, Mother went along. There was no way she wanted to stay home by herself again that day.

When they arrived in the school office, Ruthie's fever had broken. The school nurse, feeling embarrassed, swore that when the secretary had called him, Ruthie was running a temperature. Father assured her that it was okay and that they would just take her home, since they had made the trip to get her, and that she would return back to school after she had seen a doctor in a week or so.

This news made Ruthie very happy as she smiled and knew that she would be able to spend all her time with Sally again.

On the way home, Father told Ruthie that he was very worried and concerned about her. He said that there was something strange going on, and that he would find out what it was.

At the moment, Ruthie didn't respond, as she didn't understand, only being 4 years old. But she smiled again because her wish to be with Sally was coming true.

— 8 —

Tremors and More

There were just a few more days waiting until the time when Father and his new friend, Dan, were scheduled to meet at the bowling alley. I could see Mother tense up every time that Father mentioned it to any of us. That was going to be a night of fear for Mother, and at that time, I didn't know how much fear we all were about to experience.

When they arrived at the house, Ruthie couldn't wait to run up the stairs to her bedroom. She was obsessed with spending every minute with Sally and her doll house.

I, on the other hand, had just walked off the bus with Donnie and Jonathan. We were off for a break from school for a couple of weeks and were excited about Christmas. It wasn't far off. As we entered the house, we were still talking about it.

Mother and Father overheard us and Father made the comment about maybe all of us should leave the house and go back to Illinois for Christmas. At that time, after he spoke the words, the house shook again. This time, Father and all of us felt it.

"Don't be alarmed, kids. I am pretty sure that they have minor tremors here in Wisconsin. We will be fine. Go upstairs and do your homework."

Of course, we didn't argue with Father, and did as he had instructed us to do. When we started up the stairs, I stayed behind some, to see if I could overhear something that might bring me up to date on how things had really been around here.

"Connie, what was that all about?" Father asked.

"I am not sure, Tom. Remember when I asked you before if there were earthquakes or tremors here in the North Woods, and you said that you didn't know? This was stronger than the one that I had felt when I talked to you about it before. Did you feel the one that happened in here when you were talking to Ruthie this morning?"

"No, I didn't. At the time, I was too upset with her to feel anything. When I talk to Dan next, I will ask him about the tremors. I am sure they probably have noticed them as well, as he said that he has lived here his whole life."

The mention of Dan's name was now upsetting to Mother. She liked the fact that Father had a new friend, but the reminder of Father and Dan spending time together resulted in her fear of being alone in that house.

I had heard what I did and walked up the staircase to go to my room. I wanted to check on Ruthie again, so I walked quietly down the hallway and stood outside her bedroom door to listen. This is what I heard:

"Don't worry, Sally. No one will ever take me away from you again. We are more than sisters, and I will be spending my entire life here with you—and only you," Ruthie said.

Yes, there was really something to be concerned about. I would keep checking on Ruthie.

The next few days, things were fairly calm in the

old house. As long as Ruthie stayed in her room and there was no mention of leaving for Christmas, the house didn't shake. It was like that old saying, "the calm before the storm."

That night it was darker outside than I had ever seen it. The chill factor was worse than any of us had ever experienced. The electricity kept going off and on. Father had gone to find candles, as he blamed the power outage on the horrific weather that was happening.

Mother was doing dishes. As she stood at her sink, the water suddenly turned extremely cold.

"Tom, is there a way that you can go down in the basement and check the hot water heater? I am getting just really cold water."

"Yes, I will do that now." Father grabbed the flashlight and was doing what Mother asked him to do. When he got to the basement door and was ready to turn the knob, he was surprised that the door knob didn't want to turn. It had worked earlier, when he went down to get the flashlights.

"Connie, come over here," Father yelled out to Mother.

Mother, hearing this, went where Father was standing. "Yes, Tom, what is it?" she asked.

"You want to go get me my small toolbox that is out on the old porch? The door knob is stuck, or broken. I want to take it off so I can put a new knob on the door. This is the only way I can go down in the basement tonight to check anything."

As Mother was doing as Father requested, Donnie was at the kitchen sink to get drinking water when he yelled out, "Mother, the water is scalding hot now!"

Father also heard this and yelled at Mother to forget it, that he would fix the door knob in the morning.

Mother came back to the kitchen. She then told all of us that maybe things would be better in the morning. It was time for bed.

The next day was the day that Father was scheduled to go bowling with Dan. As Mother sat at the kitchen table, I could see that she was wishing that Father would cancel his plans. Again, Mother was holding her head in her hands with her elbows firmly placed on the table.

"Mama, are you all right?" I asked.

"Yes, Keli, I am fine. It is the beginning of the school's winter break for Christmas, and I guess I am just feeling a little bit overwhelmed."

"Okay, Mama," I said as I looked into her eyes. I could see that there was more to what she had said.

Father came down the stairs and walked into the kitchen, where Mother sat. "Are you all right, Connie? You look like something is troubling you," Father said as he poured himself a cup of coffee.

"Everything is good, Tom. I just have a lot to do today and am wondering what to do first," Mother replied.

"I am going to go get my toolbox and fix the door knob today. I don't know what happened, but because it has done this, I am afraid of someone getting trapped in the basement. There is a way out of it, but the kids aren't tall enough to reach the window to climb out."

"This sounds good, Tom. That could turn into a disaster if we had a house fire and one of them was downstairs and we couldn't get to him, or to her, depending on which one it was."

Then Mother said, "If you don't care, Tom, I am going to go lie down for a short time. Lately there has been too much excitement for me."

"Yes, Connie, by all means, go take a nap. I will be

up after a while to wake you up and check on Ruthie," Father replied.

It was true. With everything that had been happening, Mother was completely stressed and worn out. Today she didn't even mind going into hers and Father's bedroom alone to sleep. She was ready to give into her feelings and fear. She didn't want to live her life out in the old scary house, wondering every day if something else was going to happen.

After Mother had laid down on the bed, she was trying to relax. She had closed her eyes, but was not yet asleep. She felt a hand stroking the back of her hair. Not just once, but several times. As she turned over, she saw what appeared to be an apparition of someone lying over the top of her. How could this be happening?

She screamed out as loud as she could to Father. With him being outside on the back porch, he couldn't hear her.

The apparition went away, and Mother raised up in bed. She was more afraid than ever now and didn't know if she should tell Father. There were so many stories that he needed to hear, but she was so afraid that he would think she was needing some kind of medical help herself, because of her stories that actually did happen, but wouldn't be believable to a doctor or to Father.

So once again, instead of saying anything, she kept this information inside of herself.

By the time Father had come back through the door, Mother was sitting at the kitchen table once again. "What happened, Connie? I thought you were going to take a short nap."

"I was, Tom, but I just couldn't sleep, so I got back up to come downstairs to be with you."

"Well, maybe tonight you can go to bed a little

early. I am not sure exactly what time Dan and I will be back from bowling."

"I will see, Tom. I might wait up for you, or at least try to. I haven't heard much out of Ruthie today, and am glad that she is getting seen by the doctor tomorrow."

"Me too, Connie. Once the minor repairs are made around here and Ruthie has seen the doctor, then maybe we can make this a real home," Father said.

At that moment, Mother didn't answer back. She knew that there was no way that house could ever be a real home to any of us.

Father worked on replacing the knob until he was satisfied that it was fixed. Whereas Mother sat at the table, wondering what was next to happen in that old house, and why were there so many things happening in there that just she was noticing and not Father as well? Could it be that he was experiencing the unknown and unusual things as well, and just not telling her about them as she was not telling him?

"Tom, I have another question for you. Have you noticed anything unusual happening since the last experience you had?"

"No, Connie. I believe that I was just letting my imagination work overtime, as at the time we hadn't been here that long and everything was new to us."

"Okay, Tom," Mother replied.

"I think it would be good for you to get to know Dan's wife better, so that you can also have a good friend to go and do things with from time to time," Father said.

"I will see, Tom. You know, it isn't that easy for me to make new friends. I have the house and kids to keep me busy most of the time. Don't worry about me. I just want you to have fun tonight with Dan. I will be patiently waiting for you to return."

At the time those words came out of mother's mouth, she was just trying to reassure Father, as there was no way that she was—or would be—fine, and she would be pacing the floor instead of patiently waiting.

Father had fixed the door knob and decided that he would check on Ruthie and then come downstairs and help Mother with some of the chores that she, too, needed to do. She was starting to look somewhat pale in color herself.

When Father reached Ruthie's room, he opened her bedroom door and once again she was sitting on the floor, talking to her invisible friend. This time Ruthie saw him standing there and decided to not say a word. Maybe Sally had told her to keep quiet or she would need to go back downstairs.

"Ruthie, are you hungry? If so, come downstairs and eat."

"No. I don't want to eat," Ruthie said.

"Okay, but you know you need to eat after a while. I will leave you alone for now."

Father and Mother knew that there was no way of keeping Ruthie out of her bedroom and with the invisible Sally. The only way that this might be possible was to move her to my room. Then there would be the worry of all of these unknown things happening to me.

They had decided that until she had seen the doctor, Ruthie would continue to stay in her room. The doctor could answer more about her color, sickness, and the way to handle the invisible friend that Ruthie believed she saw and talked to every day.

— 9 —

Changes Happening

After we ate supper, Father went upstairs to get ready for Dan to arrive to pick him up. Mother had done the dinner dishes and we were instructed by Mother that even though we had no school for a couple of weeks, we would keep our normal bedtime as usual. Her words sounded strained and like she was willing to give into the commands of the old house.

I could see a change in her which worried me. I knew that Ruthie was sick and I didn't want Mother sick as well. Something had to be done about the different changes and very soon.

The clock struck 8 P.M. and Dan arrived to get Father, which was supposed to be a great night's outing for both of them.

Mother kissed Father goodbye and told him to have a good time and not to worry about her or any of us kids, that she would make sure that we were all right and taken good care of.

Father left the house, and 8:00 being our scheduled bedtime, Mother told Donnie, Jonathan and me to go to bed. There was a huge part of me that wanted to stay awake and keep an eye on not just Ruthie, but Mother as well, but instead I went to my bedroom as did Donnie and Jonathan theirs. How little did I know at the time that this would be the night that would tell the tale of the old scary house on the hill.

Mother once again sat down at the kitchen table to wait for Father to return. She was trying to convince herself that everything was going to be okay, and that she wasn't going to let little things bother her any longer. That all of this had just been her imagination and nothing more.

Mother sat at the table for an hour and then decided that it was time to go upstairs and check to see if all of us had gone to sleep. She needed to check on Ruthie as well.

I hadn't gone to sleep yet, out of worry and concern, but when I heard Mother coming up the old crackly stairs, I closed my eyes and pretended to be asleep. I didn't want her worrying about me, as I knew she had a bunch to worry about on her own, with concerns that I could see in her eyes when I looked at her.

It wasn't long before Mother had gotten to my bedroom and I knew she had already checked on Donnie and Jonathan. After me, she would be checking on Ruthie. When she opened the bedroom door to my room, I pretended to be asleep, knowing that this would give her a little peace of mind.

I heard her walking down the hallway to Ruthie's room. Mother saw the light out. When she opened the door, she saw Ruthie lying in bed, sleeping. Without the light being turned on, Mother had no idea that Ruthie was about to fall into the sleep of the dead. Ruthie was in serious condition and if she didn't get help soon, her spirit would be living with Sally in the old house forever. Sally was sucking the life out of her.

Mother closed the door and walked back down the upstairs hallway to return to the kitchen and wait for

Father. As Mother sat there, waiting, she heard what sounded to her like small children laughing and playing in the living room. Again, Mother got up from her chair and entered the living room. She could still hear the children laughing and playing, but there were no visible children in the room.

Mother, thinking that she again was just imagining this or losing her mind, went back to the table to sit and wait. When the sounds of laughter stopped, Mother believed that was all that was going to happen and that she and us children would be safe until Father returned.

More time passed, and by then even I had fallen asleep. Mother kept dozing off at the table, but was so unsettled in her mind that she was shaking herself awake. She got up to pour herself a cup of coffee, thinking that this would help keep her awake, when she heard another strange sound.

She went into the living room and saw Donnie's and Jonathan's baseball rolling slowly down each step of the staircase. When it reached the bottom step, it rolled right toward her and stopped. Once again, Mother was terrified, but knew that she needed to check to see if, for some reason, Donnie or Jonathan *wasn't* playing a trick on her, or they were just up playing baseball in their room.

She didn't hear them, but needed to make sure anyway. She climbed the staircase again and looked in their room. They were fast asleep. Not suspecting Ruthie or me, she walked down the stairs again with a horrified look on her face.

Returning to the kitchen once again to drink her coffee, she continued to hear small children playing in the living room.

Mother had no idea that Dan and Father were on

their way back to the house. They had been sitting for hours on the highway, waiting until they could turn Dan's car around, as a bad accident had occurred and no one was allowed to continue on.

Mother was holding her head in her hands again and kept hearing the children talking, playing and singing, and she couldn't take it any longer, so she got up from her chair and returned to the living room.

She was terrified, but the only thing she knew to do was to say, "I don't know who or what you are, but I am *not* going to allow myself to be afraid of you!"

The house started shaking. The television was turning itself on and off, and the children that Mother couldn't see were loudly laughing and playing, and the room felt like it was not only shaking, but spinning around.

Mother had to get us out of there, and the only thing she knew to do was to run upstairs and wake us up.

Father had returned and thanked Dan for the outing. He told him that they would do it again another time. As Dan drove away, Father noticed the house shaking severely and he knew something was wrong and that he had to help us.

Mother was upstairs and Father was trying hard to get the front door open. The knob wouldn't turn. The next plan was to go around to the back door and come into the house that way. But again, the knob would not turn.

The only thing left was the basement window that Father knew he could get through. He ran to it and kicked out the glass. He could hear Mother screaming inside the house and he felt very helpless and ashamed that he had left her and his kids in the scary old house on the hill.

After he entered the basement, Father kept a big hammer there and knew that if he couldn't get the door open, the hammer would take it out.

Again, the knob wouldn't work, so he kept hitting it until the door popped open. Father was in the kitchen, getting ready to run up the stairs to help Mother. He, too, heard the children playing and laughing and saw the television screen blinking on and off. He turned to go up the stairs and saw a big ax floating in the air.

When he ran up the stairs, he still heard Mother screaming as she was trying to get Keli's bedroom door open, so she could help with Donnie, Jonathan and Ruthie, to get them out of there. She saw Father and said, "Tom, thank God you are here! We have to leave here now!"

"I know, Connie. I will go get the boys, and then we will get Ruthie."

When Father walked into Donnie's and Jonathan's room, he saw that Jonathan had picked up a bloody knife from somewhere and was standing over Donnie's bed, getting ready to stab him with it. Jonathan was in some kind of a trance.

"Jonathan, wake up! We need to get out of this house!" He jerked the bloody knife out of his hands and by then Donnie was awake. "Let's go, boys! Grab your shoes and follow me."

Mother was still screaming as she couldn't get Keli's door open. Father told me to stand back and away from the door as he was coming through it. I did as he said. Father hit the door and it popped open. I was safe and out of the bedroom.

With the house still shaking, lights flickering off and on, we all ran to Ruthie's room. Her bedroom door opened on its own and we heard her invisible friend say, "You can't take her. She is already mine."

With this, Father said, "That is what *you* think!" He picked up Ruthie, who barely could talk, and she said, "Mama, help me."

By then, the house was shaking so badly that we could hardly walk without bumping into each other or a wall. The old stairs were shaking as well and we knew that we had limited time to get out of there. There was blood oozing down the sides of the walls upstairs.

Father yelled out, "Hurry!" We had to make it down the stairs before they collapsed, or we would be stuck upstairs and at the mercy of what we knew now were the spirits that lived there.

Father made Mother go down first with Ruthie, and then Donnie and Jonathan ran down the stairs next. When they reached the bottom stair, Father and I started running as fast as we could. By the time we reached the last stair, the staircase started to crumble and fall.

The house was shaking and the boards were so loose that we had to leave it as quickly as we could. Father knew that the only way out was through the open window in the basement.

As we ran past the kitchen sink, it had filled with blood as well and also the walls were oozing blood. When we ran down the basement stairs, we passed a wall that had broken open where Uncle Henry had placed the bodies of his family, to protect himself from the horrible crime that he had committed.

As we ran past the skeletons and skulls lying around, we knew that it was those of his wife and children. They hadn't left him, he had *killed* them and buried them in the basement.

When we reached the open window with the

house still crumbling and boards falling all around us, Father lifted Mother and Ruthie out first. To follow was Donnie, Jonathan and then me. As Father lifted himself out of the house, he yelled, "Now who has the last laugh, Sally!"

At that moment, all we heard were the moans and screams of Uncle Henry's dead family that had been trapped inside that old scary house on the hill for many years.

As we ran down the hill, we heard an explosion. The house had caught on fire, and with the gas turned on, it was blowing up.

We were safe. That was all that mattered to any of us. Ruthie's color looked normal again, and the dark circles around her eyes had gone away. She was back to normal and not with Sally, her brother and her mother in that old house.

Because of the explosion, there were fire trucks that had come to help put out the fire. Father told them to let the house burn to the ground, that he didn't care about it.

We caught a ride to Dan's house, where we stayed for a few weeks until Father could find us a different car and the means it took for us to go back to our old home in Illinois.

From what we heard at a later date, the sheriff was able to find some of the remains in the rubble of Uncle Henry's family that he had killed inside the old house. The sheriff, after having the bones sent to a lab, got the results back stating that, yes, they were those of Linda Porter, Uncle Henry's wife, Sally Porter, his daughter, and Hank Porter, his son.

Of course, Dan, Father's friend, kept in touch with Father with all the news that came available. The only thing we cared about was being able to get out of that house that was infested with spirits and not be at their mercy.

— 10 —

Fact and Reality

So here it is, twenty years later, and I decided to take a road trip back to Woodberry, Wisconsin, where I spent maybe a couple of months of my life.

The town still looked about the same as before. That is always the good part about a small town. It hardly ever changes, unlike the city that I live in now.

Dan, Father's old friend, had retired from the hardware store where Father first met him. Father and Dan continued to keep in touch, even after we moved back to our home in Illinois.

As I stand here today below the hill, I see nothing but flat land where the old house once stood. The huge trees that surrounded it have grown more and are taller than I remember them to be.

There was a reason why Mother's gloves got moved around that day, when she was certain that she had placed them under the sink on the rack. From other people who had talked to Dan after we left, apparently Uncle Henry's wife, Linda, had always laid her gloves beside the sink to dry out, and when Mother put her gloves *under* the sink, it made Linda mad. Even though Linda was dead, she was not happy that we were there. It was her home.

The incident with the extension cord that Father

had unplugged from the electrical socket before he went outside, to be found plugged in when he returned to get his sharpener, was determined from the sheriff—after Father told Dan all the occurrences that had taken place in the old house—to show from the DNA report of Linda Porter, Sally Porter and Hank Porter, that they had found fragments of what appeared to have come from a chainsaw blade and an ax.

This would explain why Father had seen an ax floating in the living room. The children playing, talking and laughing were the spirits of Sally and her brother Hank.

The odor that all of us smelled came from the decay of the rotting bones in the basement and from the three spirits of the people, whose remains had been buried behind a wall instead of being placed in the ground, which is why they watched us day and night.

None of them wanted us to leave the house alive, as they were murdered and trapped in there. They wanted us, as well, to be confined to the old house forever.

The splattered blood oozing down the walls in the kitchen and the sink could have been where Uncle Henry had killed his wife. I wanted to believe that his daughter Sally was killed in her bedroom, and that was where she wanted Ruthie to die.

The bedroom that Donnie and Jonathan shared could have also been shared by the spirit of Hank. He was more than likely stabbed to death with the same bloody knife that Uncle Henry had used to kill Sally. Sally had taken over Ruthie's mind and body, and Hank was trying to take over Jonathan's when Father entered the room.

When the baseball rolled down the stairs toward Mother, it was meant to frighten her so much that she could faint into a coma and also die there. Mother had turned very pale, like Ruthie, and was questioning what she was feeling and seeing, like the outline of a person floating above her after stroking her hair as she was lying on her bed.

With Jonathan standing over Donnie in a deep trance, holding the bloody knife, Hank was messing with Jonathan's mind and body before Father entered the room just in time, to stop it from happening.

Where I was asleep, I, too, would have been killed by Jonathan. When he realized what he had done, Hank would have talked to him, as Sally did to Ruthie, telling him to kill himself as well.

Father would have come home to all of us *dead*. Eventually he, too, would have gone insane and taken his own life as Uncle Henry had.

My thoughts are my own on actually what took place in the old house on the hill. The memories of every day there, and the horrible night that we endured, running down the upstairs hallway to run to the basement and past decayed bones that had been sawed to pieces, to fit in a tight place behind a wall, I feel the same fear that I felt that night. It was time for me to leave.

While walking back to my car, I could understand after all these years why on the first day, when the moving truck was unloading boxes and furniture, the townspeople were standing below the hill, pointing at us and whispering.

Maybe they all had witnessed the lights in the house flickering on and off, knowing that no one lived there anymore.

By coming back here and reliving the terror that we lived, I finally felt some peace. What I believed had happened in that old house, before we moved in, were questions that in my mind now had been answered.

I drove away, never to return to the North Woods of Woodberry, Wisconsin again.

PART 2

The Woman That Wouldn't Let Go

— 1 —

New Neighbor

As I lay in this hospital bed, unable to speak, with my eyes shut, I can still remember what events led up to this.

I have overheard the nurses and doctors talking with my family that patiently waits for me to wake up from the sleep that I am in.

My name is Carla Rivers. I live with my family in a suburb community in California.

This all started the day that a woman showed up at our door. I had just returned from taking my husband, Carl, to the airport. He is an airline pilot that is gone for weeks at a time.

We have a teenage daughter, a son in grade school, and a baby that is six months old.

When I heard a knock on the front door, I went to answer it with a crabby voice. "Okay, Michelle, did you forget your key again today?" I asked.

I was tired and our daughter, Michelle, was bad about leaving her house key at home, knowing that I might not be back yet from the airport when she returned from school.

When I opened the front door, I saw a tall woman who said, "Hello, I am your new next-door neighbor, Molly. I just moved into the neighborhood today."

As I extended my hand to shake hers, I said, "Hello, Molly. Happy to meet you as well. I thought you were my daughter, Michelle, who had forgotten her house key again. She is at that age where the only thing she thinks about or remembers is her boyfriend and the crowd of kids that she hangs around with. Won't you come inside, Molly? I hear my baby starting to wake up and need to go get her," I replied.

"Yes, I would love to come into your house for a while."

"I forgot to tell you my name. I am Carla Rivers. Sit down and I will be right back."

As I turned my back to go upstairs to check on Summer, my baby, Molly didn't sit down. Instead, she continued walking around downstairs, looking at everything.

When I came downstairs, I noticed her standing at the mantel, looking at a family portrait of my family that had been taken just before Christmas. As I approached Molly, she said, "Nice picture."

Being polite, but wondering why she wasn't sitting instead of standing, holding onto our portrait, I said, "Thank you, Molly. This is my family."

I had expected her to be sitting on my couch instead of checking out my house. I reached out to take back the portrait that she continued to stare at.

By then, my daughter had come through the front door with a couple of her friends. I felt that Molly had overstepped her bounds by investigating what we had downstairs. I was thinking that this was very rude and uncalled for, and that Molly was trying to familiarize herself too much with our surroundings as she continued to stare at the family portrait. I felt it was time for her to leave. I had to be as blunt as I could in asking her to come back another day.

"Molly, I hope this doesn't sound rude, but my daughter and her friends are here now, and soon my son will be here as well. I have things to take care of."

From out of nowhere, Molly said, "Your husband is very good-looking. Is he home?"

"Yes, he is, Molly, and *no*, he isn't home! I need you to just leave," I replied.

"Okay, Carla, I will leave for now."

"Yes, we will talk again soon," I told her as I was still wondering why she continued to stare at our family portrait, even after I entered the room and was trying to speak to her. She was very quick to comment on how good-looking Carl is. Was she staring at all of us, or just him?

Michelle had come down the stairs to get apples for all of her friends and herself. She walked over to me and said, "Mother, who was that woman?"

"Her name is Molly and she is our new neighbor who moved into the neighborhood today," I replied.

"The other day, when Father picked me up from school, I saw her sitting in her car behind where Father had parked his car."

"Maybe she has a son or a daughter that goes to your school, Michelle," I replied.

"Maybe," Michelle commented as she turned to go back up to her friends who were waiting on her.

As the phone rang, our son Cliff walked through the back door. I answered it, saying, "Carl, I thought you would have left by now."

"My flight was cancelled, Carla. The plane has mechanical issues. It looks like I won't be leaving now until next week. Come get me."

"I will be there shortly. Michelle is home from school and I will ask her to watch Summer until we return."

When I walked out the front door, I noticed Molly sitting on her front porch. She was facing our home. I couldn't help wondering why she was watching all of us. In spite of this, I did the neighborly thing and waved at her.

When I drove up to the pick-up lane at the airport, Carl was waiting for me. He put his luggage in the back seat and climbed into the front seat. "Hello, baby, you made good time driving here," Carl said with a smile.

Carl knew that whenever I get excited about anything, my foot becomes a piece of lead on the foot pedal. I was excited that I had more time with him.

"We have a new neighbor. She came over today to introduce herself to me. Her name is Molly. After I let her in the door, I could hear Summer upstairs and asked her to sit down as I would be right back. As I was coming down the staircase, I noticed that she was investigating all around the room to see what we had. When she heard me coming, she was at the mantel, staring at our family portrait. I tried talking to her, but she was mesmerized by the portrait of us that was taken last Christmas. She continued to stare when I was taking it from her. Oh yes, she thinks *you* are very good-looking," I said as we drove out of the airport pick-up lane.

"No worries, baby. You are the only love in my life," Carl replied.

This made me laugh and giggle at him. That was a statement that I already knew to be true. Yes, I did have a very good-looking, handsome husband that I knew loved and adored just me.

When we returned home, we found Michelle and

Cliff arguing. Summer was not with them downstairs. Carl set his luggage down and went upstairs to check on her.

"Michelle, why isn't Summer down here with you and Cliff?" I asked.

"She is fine, Mother. Geez, why do you worry all the time about it? She always cries when she needs something or wants attention."

Michelle, who was still going through the selfish, life-is-all-about-me stage, didn't really give it much thought as the words she spoke came firing out of her mouth.

With Summer being born with a severe breathing problem, I was very concerned and protective of her. All the doctors told us that it would be a good idea to watch her more than normal for her first year of life. With Michelle's attitude, I also fired back at her.

"Michelle, you know how important it is for all of us to watch your baby sister. I also know that it doesn't hurt you to continue to help us when we ask you to. Don't keep going with your attitude problem as it will only make things worse for you."

I no more than got my words out when Michelle told me that she was sorry and would help more with Summer.

Carl returned downstairs with our baby and Michelle was right, as Summer was fine.

— 2 —

Infatuation

Carl was happy to be off work for a week. It being spring, he was ready to spend the day planting a flower garden and a vegetable garden in the morning.

For now it was that time of the day for all of us to complete what we needed to before bedtime. As for Carl and I, we sat down on the couch to cuddle with each other and talk.

There was a knock at the front door. It was too late for visitors.

Carl removed his arm from around me and got up to answer the door. As he opened the door, he said, "Yes, can I help you?"

It was Molly making another appearance for the day. "Hello, I'm Molly, your new neighbor. I couldn't help but notice you in the car with Carla when she returned. I came over to introduce myself to you as I did her earlier today."

"Yes, Molly, I have heard about you from Carla. Would you like to come in and join us for a while?"

"Yes," Molly said as she walked around Carl to enter into the living room.

Again I could see that eventually she would begin staring at Carl. I was right as she wouldn't take her eyes off of him. Did Carl remind her of someone she used to know years ago, or now?

"Hello, Carla," she said.

"Hello, Molly. So, sit down and tell us about your husband and children. You should bring them over with you next time you visit, so we can meet them as well as you."

"I'm not married, Carla. I have no children," Molly replied.

Things were kind of weird now as Michelle said she had seen Molly behind Carl at her school the other day. Then again, maybe Michelle had made a mistake and it wasn't Molly at all.

"So tell us, Molly, about yourself. Where did you move from? Do you work?"

"I came from a small town in Oregon. My divorce was final last month. My husband and I were married for twelve years. So far, I am not working. I really don't need to," Molly replied.

"Wow, you are from the same state that Carl came from," I said as I looked at her. With every word that came out of her mouth, it was like she was just in the room with Carl. She couldn't take her eyes off of him.

Cliff had returned downstairs to talk to Carl. "Father, there might be an hour of sunlight left. Do you want to go outside and kick the football around for a while?" Cliff asked.

"Sure, son. We can do that," Carl replied.

"Okay, that's great," Cliff said as he went running toward the door.

I continued to watch Molly as she smiled at Cliff and Carl. Something definitely was not right with her.

After Carl and Cliff walked out the door, Molly said, "Maybe I should leave now. I have something to do before it gets dark."

"Yes, Molly, I too have things to do." My sentence

wasn't even finished and Molly had left the house, shutting the door behind her.

I was very convinced that the only reason she had come here tonight was so she could see my husband, Carl.

Summer was sleeping peacefully, so I walked to the window to watch Cliff and Carl kick the ball around. Molly was standing close to Carl with her hand on Cliff's shoulder. She was holding the football. Both Cliff and Carl were smiling at her.

I then went to the door and opened it. Molly saw me do this and handed Cliff the ball. She mumbled something to them and walked away.

Giving her plenty of time to cross the street, I went outside to talk to Carl.

"Cliff, your father will be throwing you the ball soon. Right now I need to talk to him in private."

"Okay, Mother," Cliff said as I then took Carl's hand so he could follow me to an area where Cliff couldn't hear what I said.

"What was all that about, Carl?" I asked.

"What was *what* about, Carla?"

"I opened the curtain so I could watch you and Cliff. I saw Molly talking to both of you. What did she say?" I asked.

"Carla, don't tell me you are jealous," Carl said with a slight snicker in his voice.

"You can laugh if you want, Carl, but there is something very odd about Molly."

"All she said was that she played football with her little brother when they were younger, and she asked Cliff to hand her the ball so she could show him how to hold it, so it would go further when he threw it. That was why we were smiling at her, Carla. Are you all right? You have never acted like this before!"

"I don't know, Carl. It just appears to me that she only came here to see you tonight. She is too friendly."

"Carla, everyone that lives or has lived in Oregon is very friendly. Maybe she is just that way. Give her a chance, Carla. I am sure you are just overreacting," Carl said as he walked back to Cliff.

I walked back into the house to stay and to check on Summer. She was sleeping, so I sat down on the couch to wait for Cliff and Carl to return to the house. When they did return, they were laughing and talking. Cliff went upstairs and Carl sat down next to me on the couch. Once again, he put his arm around me. I laid my head on his shoulder.

Carl had picked up the remote and turned the television on. We were there to stay until bedtime.

The next morning as I stood at the stove, cooking breakfast, Carl and Cliff smelled the bacon cooking and had to come downstairs to eat. Summer was in her high chair, smiling as Carl tickled the bottoms of her feet.

Michelle was talking on the phone to a friend and Cliff was still talking to Carl about how he now knew the correct way to hold the football.

"Cliff, you were holding it right after all. Don't listen to what Molly told you to do. She was just being nice, and trying to get to know you and me better," Carl responded to Cliff.

"Okay, but I like her," Cliff replied.

Carl noticed that my eyebrow had raised some when I heard the name Molly, and felt the need to correct Cliff.

"What do you have planned to do today, since you are off from work, besides putting in a couple of gardens?" I asked Carl.

"I think this is going to take the full day, so nothing else by me has been planned. Tomorrow I thought it would be fun if we drive down to the beach with the kids and have some fun in the sun together," Carl answered.

"Yes, this sounds like a fun couple of days." I wanted to add, "if Molly stays away ..." but chose not to.

Breakfast was ready and it was time to eat. Afterwards, Carl excused himself from the table and left the house to get everything he needed to start the projects he wanted to complete before the end of the day.

Michelle had left the house to pick up a friend, and Cliff went upstairs to finish school work.

I was clearing the dishes from the table when I heard a knock at the front door. There was a package lying on the step. The mailman, seeing that I had heard the knock and opened the door, waved and drove away.

Shutting the door, I returned to Summer and the work that I needed to complete before going outside to help Carl as much as I could.

Molly had been watching the house again and had made her way over to talk, but not to me. When I opened the door to go outside and help, I noticed her hunched over the flower bed, talking to Carl. Besides knowing everything about football, was she also an expert on planting flowers?

So I walked over to them. "Molly, what brings you back here again today?" I asked.

"I saw Carl planting more flowers. I happen to have a drawer full of flower and vegetable seeds and thought that he might be able to use them," she replied.

"Well, thank you, Molly, for wanting to help, but I think we are all right without them."

At that moment, she gave me a sideways smile. "Okay, Carla," she responded.

"Carla, it is okay. Molly was just trying to help."

I was not comforted by the fact that Carl was defending Molly and her actions. Without showing a harsh facial expression that would be very noticeable, I said, "Okay, Molly. Thank you."

By then I needed to return to the house to check on my baby again. I had decided to back away when Molly came over here. I knew that before long Carl would notice that Molly was infatuated with him. He would tell her that he is in love with his wife and to stay away from him.

— 3 —

What's So Great about Molly?

When Carl completed the flower garden, Molly was right beside him, talking and smiling as Carl smiled and talked to her. It looked like with or without my permission, Carl had made a new friend. Now it was the waiting game to see how long it would take Carl to be sick of her following him around.

I continued to stay in the house, working and waiting for Carl to be done outside. Michelle and her friend were upstairs playing music, and Cliff went outside to be around his dad and Molly. It was going to be a day when I would be sitting alone, playing and talking to Summer, and not Carl.

When the excitement was over, Cliff and Carl returned to the house to shower and get ready for supper.

Again, Cliff expressed his feelings. "Dad, I sure do like Molly. She knows how to do everything."

I continued to cook and didn't say a word. Michelle's friends had left. Michelle entered the room and said, "That woman is becoming part of the furniture."

With a sideways smile and a snicker under my breath, even though I, too, agreed with her, I said, "Michelle, it isn't nice to talk about our new neighbor like that. I'm pretty sure that when the newness wears off, everything will go back to the way it was before."

At least that is what I wanted to believe, but little did I know that it was only going to get worse.

Cliff and Carl had joined us in the kitchen, with Carl thinking that he was in trouble for spending so much time with Molly today. He didn't know what to say, so he remained quiet until I said, "Kids, Dad and I want to take you to the beach tomorrow."

This was the ice breaker, as then Carl replied that he had already mentioned our outing to Cliff when they were outside. Michelle, loving the beach, was excited.

When supper was over, Michelle and Cliff left the room. I didn't bring up Molly. She had been too much a part of our day as it was already pretty much ruined because of her persistence with her infatuation over Carl. Tonight I just wanted our day to end with a loving, peaceful evening with my husband.

Like every night when Carl was home and we were alone, we snuggled on the couch together, watching TV or a movie before we went to bed.

When the sun was up in the morning, we were up and dressed, ready to leave the house for a fun-filled day at the beach for all of us.

As we passed by Molly's house, I noticed that her garage door was up and her car was gone. Perhaps she had made another friend to annoy and antagonize for that day. I was laughing silently to myself and didn't say a word.

When we arrived at the beach, there were many other people that had the same plans as we did for fun that day. We went running toward the water and—who should appear, but *Molly*—all decked out in a very skimpy bathing suit!

Apparently, she had overheard Carl telling Cliff

about our plans for today. She was talking to us like we were her long lost cousins. "I see you made it!" Molly said.

"Yes!" Cliff said as he grabbed her hand. "I'm so happy to see that you came here too." Again, Cliff was ecstatic to see her.

"Well, it looks like we are all here to have a day of fun, so let's get to it," Molly replied.

With me, I had carried a beach blanket plus an umbrella to protect Summer from the sun. It was starting to look like my day was going to be spent sitting and watching everyone *else* have fun, as all of them took off running and laughing to the ocean, to swim and play.

Cliff had brought his beach ball and all of them were playing in the water. Cliff took the ball and batted it to Molly. She then hit it back to him. The ball was going back and forth when Michelle and Carl swam over to join in the fun.

Molly turned around and started splashing water on them. If I didn't know better, I would think that all four of them were one happy family. Even with seeing all of this, I didn't want to come across to Carl as being the jealous wife, so I continued to sit in the sun with Summer.

After hours had passed, Carl, Cliff, Michelle and Molly came back to where I was sitting.

"What a fun day," Molly said as she smiled and talked to Carl.

I was happy that they'd had a fun day. Carl didn't respond back to Molly's comment. He had to know that all of this was bothering me, but again I didn't say a word other than in my mind, I kept thinking about Molly, the woman that wouldn't let go.

Before going home, Carl took us all out to a burger

place. I know he was feeling somewhat guilty because of the crappy day that I had just had, and he was trying to smooth over the situation of the day at the beach.

By the time we returned home, it was dark and late. Michelle and Cliff went upstairs to bed as Summer, Carl and I did the same. This would not be a night of snuggling together on the couch.

The next morning, as I sat downstairs, waiting for everyone to wake up, I again heard a knock on the door. When I opened it, I saw Molly there, holding a big box of donuts.

"Carla, I hope I am here before you started cooking breakfast. Cliff mentioned to me yesterday that it had been a while since you had brought home any donuts," Molly said as she looked toward the stairs.

She had awakened Carl, Cliff and Michelle. Of course, Cliff was happy to see her *and* the donuts. Michelle was starting to like her as well, and was talking to her about the fun day at the beach.

Carl was sitting on the couch with his pajama bottoms on, with an open bathrobe. Molly wouldn't take her eyes off of him. How did Carl not see this infatuation that she had for him, or *did* he and he liked it?

I felt like I was focusing on my feelings too much at the moment. I was wondering if maybe I wasn't showing Carl enough attention. With Summer being sick so much, I—without meaning to—was feeling like I might be failing as a lover to him. This I would need to change.

Wanting to show Carl affection in front of Molly, I gave him a long good morning kiss, one that I hoped irritated Molly.

Molly did notice this and her reaction was strange. She looked at me like I had just given *her* husband a long, passionate kiss. To my dismay, Carl failed to see this. I would now be fighting fire with fire where Molly was concerned.

Cliff, being a kid, didn't understand what was happening. He just knew that he really liked Molly and the donuts. After he downed four of them, he asked her if she wanted to walk with him to school. He had grown very attached to her.

"Sure, Cliff, I would love to walk you to school," Molly replied.

Of course, this made Cliff's day. He took her hand and walked out the door. Cliff, being very young, also asked her something else that made me shed a tear.

"Is it okay if I tell some of my friends that you are my mommy?"

"Sure you can, Cliff. I would love to be your mommy." This, I'm sure, was something that Molly was waiting for. She would love to take over my spot in this house. Molly had won Cliff's heart and soon she would be targeting Michelle as well, while still smiling at Carl. In her mind, it was one down and three to go, as she wanted Carl at the top of her list.

Maybe Michelle was right the other day when she was talking to me about being so overly protective of Summer. In her way, she wanted me to know that I was just not Summer's mother, but hers and Cliff's as well.

I had to make some changes with my priorities. My world would crumble to the ground if I didn't.

Carl, seeing me in deep thought, said, "Are you all right with Molly walking Cliff to school?"

I said, "Yes, Carl, he is just a kid with a new friend."

— 4 —

Is This Still My Home?

I was the one who needed to put my family back together again in every way possible. As for Molly, I was sure she was counting on me *not* being able to.

Michelle came down the stairs and asked if she could take my car to school. Of course, I told her that she could.

"Thank you, Mother. So glad we all had fun at the beach. Sure did seem strange, though, that Molly was there on the same day that we were," Michelle said as she picked up her school books to leave the house.

I had some shopping to do, so I asked her to drop me off. I would take a cab back home when I was finished.

Again, I gave Carl a very passionate kiss. In reply to my kiss, he said, "Thank you. I could get used to that." I knew that I had scored points and hit a home run.

When we drove away, I made it a point again to look at Molly's house. Standing at the window, Molly was also watching us, to see who all was in my car. Now I needed to see if she would go to the house to get Carl alone and jump on that opportunity.

I was finished in town. I took a cab back to the house, and the driver asked if I needed help with what

I had bought. I replied to him that my husband would come out to pay him and get what I couldn't carry myself.

As I was walking toward the front door, I could hear talking and laughter coming from the living room. When I opened the door, Molly was sitting on the couch, holding Summer and talking to Carl—playing with *my* baby.

"Oh, you made it home, Carla," Molly said. At that time I was so aggravated that I wanted to say, "You are right, Molly. It *is* my home. Carl *is* my husband, and Cliff, Michelle and Summer are *my* kids. So don't let the door hit you in the ass on the way out." What I wanted to say and what I *did* say were totally different, however.

"Yes, Molly, I am home now," was what I chose to say, doing as Carl had instructed, to be nice to her. I would give her a chance that she, I knew, didn't deserve.

"Carl, would you go get the rest of the bags and pay the driver?" I asked, wondering why he continued to sit on the couch next to Molly and not help me. I kept wondering what was so charming about Molly.

When Carl went outside, I walked over to Molly and took Summer from her arms. When I did that, she got up from the couch and asked me if I wanted a cup of coffee. All of this was very strange and I felt like a guest in my own home.

Feeling somewhat picked on and irritated at the same time, I said abruptly, "No, Molly."

Carl had entered the house and was on his way to the kitchen with the food that I had gotten in town. Of course, Molly followed him.

This is what I heard ...

"I will be looking forward to your arrival soon,"

Molly spoke.

"Yeah, I'll be over there in a little while," Carl replied back.

Molly then came out of the kitchen and walked past me again, without saying a word, and left. I waited a minute to make sure she wouldn't be coming back through the door, and when I was convinced that she was gone, I went into the kitchen to put the food from the store away. I saw Carl opening and shutting drawers.

"What are you looking for?" I asked.

"I'm trying to find my pipe wrench. I need to go over to Molly's and fix her kitchen sink."

"Can't she hire a plumber?" I asked.

"Probably, but she asked me to do it and I told her that I would," Carl replied.

Again, the mean side of me wanted to say, "Oh yeah, if she asked you to jump, would you ask how high?" Instead, I just said, "Okay." I could see that he was determined to do this, in spite of what I said.

As I continued to put the food away, he continued to search through all the cupboards and drawers for his pipe wrench. When he finally did find it, he came over to where I was standing and gave me somewhat of a little peck on the cheek as a goodbye kiss.

"I'll see you later," said Carl.

"Okay, I will see you later." Again I knew I would be spending my day alone with Summer in our home, waiting for his return. Time was running out on our alone time, as he only had three or four days left before he would be gone for a while.

If things didn't change with Molly, the woman that wouldn't let go, I would do whatever I had to do or say to her, to get her out of our lives forever.

Hours passed as I paced the floor, holding onto

Summer, still waiting for Carl's return. I had even gone to the window to look across the street, to see if Molly or Carl was visible to watch. I saw nothing.

Before I knew it, Cliff and Michelle were back from school. They were asking me where their dad was. All I could say was, "He's at Molly's, fixing her sink."

All they said was, "That is nice of Father to do this for her." Yes, it might be nice of him, as Carl was a very nice person, who always tried to see the best in everyone. This time, though, in these particular circumstances, I was afraid that he was getting himself into a situation that wasn't going to turn out good for him, or for us.

Just before I called to Cliff and Michelle to come downstairs to prepare to eat supper, Carl came home. His clothes were dirty and he announced that he needed to go take a shower before he would be at the table to eat. With the greasy clothes, I was sure that Carl had taken care of Molly's sink and pipes, but not in the fashion that *she* wanted him to. All I could do was stand there and smile.

As Carl was showering, I received a phone call from my Aunt Mary, telling me that it was very important for me to go to Salinas. Mother had tripped and broken her foot. The doctor needed my help to convince her that she would need surgery on it. My father had passed away years ago, and since I was Mother's only child, I had to be the one to sign the consent form to have the surgery done, if Mother's stubbornness continued.

This was not a good time for me to be gone, but knowing if I left early enough in the morning, I would make it a point not to stay in Salinas, but be home by tomorrow night.

I saw Carl coming down the stairs. I needed to tell

him about this right away, in case I would need to call the doctor back and reschedule my appearance for a different day.

"Carl, Aunt Mary called me. Mother has tripped and broken her foot. She is refusing surgery and the doctor wants me there to convince her that she needs to have it. I will leave early enough tomorrow morning, where I will be back tomorrow night. Do you need Michelle to stay home from school to help you with Summer?"

"No, Carla. I can take care of Summer by myself."

"Okay, then. I will not spend the night there." I was wishing that Carl would bring Summer and come with me, and knowing otherwise that Molly would be there to keep him company the whole day until after I returned.

Every time I looked out the living room window, Molly was standing at her window, watching our house. In spite of everyone's trust in her, thinking that she was just a nice, lonely lady across the street, I could feel—and I knew—that she was not all that nice. There was something odd about her, and the whole situation with her not letting go of us.

Tonight, instead of Carl and I snuggling again on the couch, we just went to bed. I didn't like the way our lives had changed.

— 5 —

Pizza, Anyone?

The day started early for me. Today would be a warm day again. I would much rather be sitting on the couch, snuggling with Carl, or doing something fun together. Our time together was, and always has been, very precious to me.

Instead, I left the house before it was light outside in hopes that Molly wouldn't see me leave. It was still dark and she should still be asleep. When I looked over at her window, I didn't see her.

Regardless of what I came home to, I had to help my mother today. She needed me there.

When I arrived in Salinas, Aunt Mary was waiting for me. I talked to Mother about her injury, and after much discussion, by early afternoon I had convinced her to take care of business, and have the surgery done and over with. I was on my way home.

Many hours later, as I drove into the driveway and got out of my car, I once again heard laughter coming from the living room of our home. As I opened the door, I saw Carl, Michelle, Cliff and Molly sitting in different places, eating pizza that had been ordered in.

I could see that Summer was not with them, and so I dropped my jacket and ran upstairs to check on her. She was okay and fast asleep.

When I walked down the stairs and entered the living room, Carl could see that something was bothering me. I had tried to understand and accept Molly as my friend—even as dysfunctional as I knew our relationship would be. But again, I thought by now that Carl would have gotten tired of her being around him all the time.

I think she could see that I was about to lose it, and she didn't offer me coffee or pizza in my own home. Instead, she said, "I am leaving now, but will see you tomorrow."

She walked out the door. Michelle and Cliff had finished eating and left the room.

Carl said, "How is Mother?"

"I was able to talk her into the surgery."

"What day is it?"

With everything that had happened and what I had come home to yet again, I wanted to say, "What do you care? You should have come with me instead of entertaining Molly."

Like the other times, it was just a straight answer of, "Her surgery is the day you go back to work. I will drop you off at the airport, and then leave for Salinas from there. I will ask Mrs. Hearrington to come here to watch Summer while I am gone."

"Okay, Carla. Let's go to bed. I know you are tired," Carl replied.

This would make the third night that Carl and I hadn't snuggled in front of the TV before bedtime. All I could say to him was, "Okay."

The next day would be the last day that Carl had off, and I was hoping that it, being a Friday with the kids in school, I could call Mrs. Hearrington and ask her if she would come over Friday and Saturday to watch Summer. Tomorrow, maybe Carl and I could leave and be alone, unless Molly caught wind of it first.

"Carl, is it all right if, when I call Mrs. Hearrington early tomorrow morning, I ask her if she will watch Summer not just Saturday, but also tomorrow as well, so that we can spend the day together alone, without the kids?"

"Yes, Carla. That would be nice," Carl replied.

I turned the light off for the night and we went to sleep.

I had called and made arrangements with Mrs. Hearrington to come over, so that Carl and I could spend the day alone. My only hope was that Molly wouldn't show up at the door to spoil it for us.

Michelle and Cliff had left for the day. Mrs. Hearrington was on her way. No sign of Molly. It was a *go*, and at last Carl and I were loaded in the car and on our way to a fun park alone, without interruptions, so we could finally have our one day of fun alone together.

"Carla, now that you know Molly better, have you changed your opinion of her?"

Here we were—happy, laughing and talking—and Carl chose to mention Molly!

"I am sorry, Carl, but I still feel like, in her mind, there is something going on with her. She might be a lonely woman, but she should go meet the other neighbors too."

Not wanting to ruin our day, I left it at that.

"I see the look in your eyes when you see her with me. I just want to tell you that you have nothing to worry about where I am concerned."

This was something that I didn't expect, but needed to hear from Carl. It had just been a hectic week for us. Maybe I should stop imagining things and really get to know Molly better. After all, she was from Oregon, the "friendly" state, as Carl had mentioned.

Time flew by for us that day. Carl won me two stuffed bears from a shooting booth, and we had a blast riding several rides together. We both felt like teenagers again, sharing a box of popcorn and cotton candy. Our day together was wonderful and I hated to see it end.

On the way home, we held hands and leaned over to kiss each other several times.

When we went past Molly's home, she wasn't there. What she was preparing for, I would find out about after Carl had left on his flight out tomorrow. This time he would be away for a couple of weeks.

Michelle and Cliff were home from school, and Mrs. Hearrington was letting me know she would be back extra early in the morning. This would be a night of fun, and I told Carl to order a large pizza with everything on it. I was trying to make up for a week of the wrath of Molly.

Carl lit candles, and we turned out the lights. After Michelle and Cliff went upstairs, Carl and I once again snuggled together on the couch until we both went to sleep, holding each other as we watched a movie.

After a peaceful night of rest, all of us were up early. Michelle and Cliff told their dad goodbye and left for school. Mrs. Hearrington had arrived to watch Summer. Carl was dressed in his pilot uniform. He picked up his bag and we were on our way to take him to the airport.

When we drove past Molly's house, she was watching from the window. She could see Carl in the driver's seat, all dressed up, and she knew that he would be gone for a while. Now came the test, to see if she would come over to the house to get to know me.

At the airport where I parked to let Carl out, it was a repeat of what we had done many times. We stood close to each other, holding and kissing each other until he had to leave. As he walked away, he continued to wave and throw kisses at me as I was also doing back to him.

That was the last time I saw Carl.

I hear his voice when he comes into my hospital room, and the cries from Carl, Michelle and Cliff. All I can do is wait to wake up.

After I drove away from the airport, I thought I saw Molly in her car, following me. But in California, so many people drive the same kinds of cars and I couldn't be sure. My mind could have been playing tricks on me.

I drove to Salinas and picked up Aunt Mary, to return to the hospital to wait it out while Mother had her surgery. Still a long day ahead for me.

Hours passed and I kept watching the clock, wondering what part of the world Carl was in now. He said he would call me later tonight.

After waiting, the doctor returned to the area where Aunt Mary and I had been sitting, to give us the good news about the surgery going well. They would be keeping Mother overnight and Aunt Mary said she would stay with her until she could function again on her own. This was good news for me, as I was needed at my home with my family.

I made a couple of stops before returning home. As I drove past Molly's house, I could see that at the time being, her car was parked in her garage.

Shortly after entering the house, Mrs. Hearrington heard me coming to the door. She was walking down the stairs, carrying Summer. She announced that a lady by the name of Molly had stopped by to get Michelle and Cliff. She had asked them if they wanted to help her make cookies, and she also said that she was a very good friend of the family and she knew it would be all right with me.

I wasn't okay with it, but told Mrs. Hearrington that it was all right, and then I thanked her for helping us out both days.

When she left, all I could do was wait for Carl to call me, and for Michelle and Cliff to come home.

Coming through the front door, Michelle said, "Mother, you should see the inside of Molly's house. It is so organized and beautiful. We had so much fun over there, helping her make cookies today. She seems really nice."

Cliff spoke, "Yes, I *love* Molly."

This was a strange thing for Cliff to say, as normally he only "liked" other people instead of *loving* them. As for Michelle, I knew that she was hyped up on cookies, as she loved making and eating them.

The phone was ringing and it was Carl calling me. My focus was totally on him.

"Carl, I'm so glad you called me. Also that you had a safe trip today."

"The flight went well, Carla. I was told that I will be coming back home for a couple days on Tuesday. I will call again, to give you more instructions and the time of my arrival."

"That is great, Carl! I will see you soon."

After the call, I made sandwiches for supper. I knew Cliff and Michelle wouldn't be hungry from all the cookies they had eaten at Molly's.

After we ate, I locked the door and we went to bed.

— 6 —

Crossing the Line

The next morning, I was more relaxed than I had been since Molly came into our lives. It had been two days since I had seen her, and I was loving it.

Michelle and Cliff were on their way to school. How little did I know at that time that Molly was taking them. This part both of them failed to mention when they came home last night.

I was going to try to accept the fact that Molly was our neighbor and the reality that she would be running in and out of here from time to time. Like Michelle had plainly stated that day, Molly was a piece of furniture.

I also wanted to believe that Molly would eventually stop chasing after my husband, as she probably was a lonely woman, but Carl was not available to her, or for her. It was very apparent that she was trying to win my children over.

As the day progressed, there was a knock on the door. I recognized it as the knock of Molly. When I answered the door, she had a plate of cookies.

"Carla, I brought over some cookies for you, Michelle and Cliff."

"Thank you," I said, trying my hardest to be nice to her.

"By the way, I took Michelle and Cliff to school today."

"What!" I said.

"Yes, I wanted to take them. Poor babies taking the bus or walking every day. I was sure that you wouldn't mind."

"Next time, Molly, ask me first," I told her.

She didn't reply, but went to the kitchen to fix herself some coffee. She had made herself at home in my house. As she returned to the living room, she was again walking over to the mantel to look at the family portrait of my family. Was she picturing herself with Carl, Cliff, Michelle and Summer instead of me with them?

"Molly, why do you stare at our family portrait when you come over here?" I asked as I figured that was a reasonable question she might want to answer.

"Maybe because we look so nice in it."

There was no *we* and now she had creeped me out. I knew she was odd, but even that was too much for me to absorb.

"Molly, I think you should set your coffee cup down and leave my house now! I have a lot to do today!"

"Well, okay, Carla. I will see you soon," she replied with a wild look in her eyes.

This time when she left the house, all I could think of was to take Summer, lock the door and leave the house for the day. The thought of pulling Michelle and Cliff out of school, and not coming back here until Carl arrived home, was something that had entered my mind. Then I thought that maybe instead of her referring to herself in the portrait, she might have meant to say, "you" instead of "we." The wild look in her eyes was still standing, and it was time to leave.

I had already started out the door and was on my way to somewhere. I wouldn't be home before the kids were expected here.

About twenty minutes before I knew they were scheduled to return, Summer and I finally did come back home. I parked my car, looking in every direction possible, to make sure that Molly, in her craziness, wasn't going to sneak up on me when I climbed out.

I got Summer out of her car seat and walked to the front door.

After I had unlocked it and gone inside, I could not believe my eyes. The living room furniture had been rearranged! The only one I knew of that would have done this was Molly. How had she gotten into the house? I knew the front door was locked by me when Summer and I left today.

Maybe, for some reason, Cliff or Michelle had forgotten to lock the back door. Our privacy had been invaded, as Molly had no right to enter my home with no one here.

I put Summer upstairs in her crib and came downstairs. I picked up the phone to call the police to report her, and as I was dialing the numbers, I changed my mind. If I did this without talking to Carl and getting his permission, there was a chance that he, Cliff and Michelle would be upset with me and not understand. Molly had all of them fooled into thinking she was a nice, lonely woman who just wanted to help. I, on the other hand, looked at her as being NUTS. I put the phone down. She was an interfering, trouble-making woman that wouldn't let go.

When Michelle walked in the house, she said, "What are you doing, Mother, changing the furniture around?"

"No, Michelle, I am putting it back the way it was."

"What do you mean?" Michelle asked.

"Molly came in here today and moved our furniture

around while I was gone. I know you like her a lot, but this kind of behavior frightens me, Michelle."

"It is okay, Mother. I will help you put it back the way it was. After this, I will stay away from Molly." Michelle had spoken, and even she had seen a different side that was weird and highly unusual.

Before we were finished, Cliff had returned home. I told him what I had told Michelle, and he was not so eager to hear what I had to say.

"Mother, I like Molly. I don't want to stay away from her!"

Cliff was a little boy with a huge desire to want to keep Molly as his friend, in spite of what was best for him, or what she did today.

After the supper meal was over with, the phone rang. Carl was calling.

When I answered it, he said, "Carla, I called to let you know that I will be home very late tomorrow night. When you are tired, just go to bed, and I will try not to wake you up when I come into the bedroom. I will have a taxi take me to the house. Is everything okay there?"

"Yes, we are good. I will probably be asleep when you do get home. Please have a safe flight back."

I could have gone into detail about what Molly had done while he was away. If I did this, it would all be on his mind, and flying a plane to get home safely was more important to me at the moment.

Michelle and Cliff had already gone to their rooms for the night, and I turned off all the lights. It also was time to make sure that every door and entrance to this house was locked.

Since I was still pretty wound up from everything that had transpired, I put Summer into her playpen and sat down on the couch with the remote to watch a movie. The curtains were closed. I was sure that Molly was pondering over what she had done, and wondering what my reaction had been.

Finally I was relaxed and in my comfort zone. It wasn't long after that when I was sound asleep.

When I woke up, realizing that I had spent the entire night sleeping on the couch, I turned off the TV and was stretching as I walked to the kitchen to get Summer some milk and coffee for myself.

Soon I heard Michelle and Cliff coming down the stairs. Today Michelle was worried about me and asked if I needed her to stay home with me. Of course, I told her no and that I would be okay.

Cliff was still upset with my orders, telling him to stay away from Molly. He did have an attitude problem.

"Good morning, Cliff," I said with a smile.

"Okay, Mother. Are you going to make Molly move away now?" he asked.

"Cliff, I know you really like Molly. She has done things that I don't approve of, and I know your father wouldn't approve of her actions either. For now, I am very serious about you staying away from her."

Cliff, with a pouty look, picked up his school books and was getting ready to leave the house to take the school bus to school when he found the cookies sitting on the end table. He took some and walked out the door.

I asked Michelle if she would keep an eye on Cliff, to make sure that he didn't make a detour to Molly's house before the school bus arrived. She said that she would, and like Cliff, grabbed cookies before leaving. I couldn't tell them not to eat the cookies. After all, it wasn't the fault of the cookies that all of this had happened. They did love homemade cookies.

When Michelle left the house, I locked the front door. I had made up my mind at the time that I wasn't going to answer it, no matter how many times Molly knocked. I wasn't going to let her ruin my day. At the time I was thinking this, it sounded good and felt good, but I no more than thought this when I heard Molly knocking on the door. I was still steaming from everything that had occurred, but went ahead and answered it anyway.

As usual, Molly walked right in as if she owned the house.

"Oh, Carla, I see you didn't like the way I arranged the furniture. I also see the cookies were a welcome treat," Molly said with a huge, almost scary smile.

I had been holding back for some time and finally I couldn't any longer.

"Molly, I have something to say, and you will listen. From the first day you came over here, I have noticed so many things about you. It's odd how I practically had to jerk the family portrait from your hands the first day as you stood at the mantel, staring at it. When you met Carl, you couldn't keep your eyes off of him. You keep watching our home as I see you standing at your living room window, day and night, before we close the curtains.

"You came over here to help Carl plant both gardens with seeds that you knew he wouldn't reject. It was what *you* wanted to grow, knowing that I wanted to help him. When you heard that we were going to have a family outing, you couldn't wait for us to get to the beach, so you could occupy my family's time with all of your cutesy games in the ocean, again knowing that it was our family time together.

"Also, you have tried to win my children's love away from me by sitting with Carl, Michelle, Cliff and my baby Summer. Playing football with Cliff and Carl in the street, trying to make Cliff think that you are some kind of an expert on throwing the football, and holding it a certain way for long passes. Coming here and staying all day with my husband and baby, to stay longer so you could eat pizza with all of them until I got home. Talking Carl into fixing your kitchen sink pipe, to keep him away from me.

"You, taking Michelle and Cliff to your house to make cookies, and to school without asking me first. Plus I know that was you who followed me when I took Carl to the airport. Then, after you helped yourself to coffee in my kitchen, returning to the living room to once again stare at my family's portrait, saying that we look nice in it.

"Molly, there is no *we* where you are concerned. I came home after leaving here to get Summer and myself away from you, because I think you are very odd and it's unusual for me to come home to see that my furniture has been adjusted and moved around to where *you* want each item to be placed.

"Molly, you are a very bothered, weird, odd woman that doesn't want to let go. I can't take any more of your interference with my family any longer. I have talked to Michelle and Cliff, telling them to stay away from you. I am telling Carl all about this when he returns. I know that he will feel the same way that I do and want you completely out of our lives forever.

"So, what I am now saying to you, Molly, is to get out of my house, forget about all of us, and don't ever come back!"

"Oh, Carla, you shouldn't have told Cliff and Michelle what you did. You will be sorry if you tell Carl anything. I will make you pay." Molly had another slight smile on her face. Her eyes went wild and out of control from all the anger. She jerked open the front door and said again, "I will make you *pay* for this!"

I slammed the door in her face and locked it. It had been some time since anyone had made me as mad as she did. As for her threats, they didn't bother me, not knowing at the time that I should be extremely terrified.

Now it was time for me to sit in my house with my baby Summer, and wait for Michelle and Cliff to arrive home.

— 7 —

Craziness and Terror

While waiting, I continued to watch out the living room window until I knew that Michelle and Cliff were home safe and sound. Carl would be home tonight —late—and I couldn't wait. I had so much to tell him.

When Cliff came through the front door, he had Michelle close behind him. I felt as if she also had noticed things that Molly was doing, but just didn't want to imagine that she could be right. As with Carl and Cliff, she wanted to like Molly, thinking that what she was doing was out of loneliness and being a divorced woman that just wanted friends.

"Cliff, would you take the trash out to the dumpster for me?"

"I guess, Mother," he replied with still somewhat of an attitude problem. I know that when Carl had the chance to speak with him, he would be able to make Cliff understand things that I couldn't.

Michelle, not trusting her little brother, said, "I will help you, Cliff." I'm sure she was thinking that after he took the garbage out, he might go over to Molly's house to see how she was, even though he knew he wasn't supposed to.

Soon everyone was in the house again. I was starting supper, and Cliff and Michelle were playing board games on the living room floor with Summer watching, laughing and kicking her feet in excitement with them being there with her.

There still was no sign of Molly for the rest of the day. My hopes were that she was out of our lives forever.

As it got later in the day, Cliff and Michelle went to their rooms for the night. I, on the other hand, sat in the living room alone. I had taken Summer up to her crib for the night. The anticipation of Carl coming home that night, and the thought of staying up to wait for him, was my plan. But the later it got, the more tired I became until I needed to go to bed.

I was sure that I would wake up the minute he came into the room.

I checked all the locks again on the doors, and started up the stairs, turning out lamps and light switches as I went. It didn't take me long before I, too, was fast asleep.

Not being sure of the time, as I had been asleep, I heard the bedroom door open and shut. The street light was shining through the bedroom window, like it did every night. Seeing the silhouette of a person, my guess was that Carl was home. I turned over on my back with my eyes closed, to wait for him to undress and crawl into bed with me.

At that very moment, I felt someone holding my arms down on my chest. I couldn't move. This startled me so much that I also couldn't breathe. Immediately I opened my eyes.

Standing over me was none other than Molly, holding a knife to my throat, and telling me to be quiet and not scream or say a word. She was much taller and stronger than I was, with large hands for a woman.

I tried struggling to get loose, and again she said, "Don't scream, Carla. If you do, I will hurt Summer. Stop struggling as it won't do you any good!"

"Molly, why are you doing this? Why did you choose *my* family to terrorize? Have you hurt Michelle and Cliff?" I cried frantically.

"I haven't hurt them. They are *my* children, Carla. Why would I hurt my own children?" she replied with another crazy, wild look in her eyes.

By then, Molly was leaning tighter on my chest. My fear became even stronger. I was trapped under the blankets, with my arms pinned tightly to my chest. I couldn't move.

If I screamed, I knew that she would stab me and also my baby.

Wanting her to leave, I said, "Molly, if this has something to do with Carl and you being together, just tell me … and I will leave and not come back."

"Carla, what happened with Carl and me started years ago. He doesn't recognize me now as my ex-husband gave me a different face. I went to school with Carl. I have loved him for many years. We dated and while he was messing around on me with my best friend, we spoke our undying love for one another. Even though he cheated on me, I knew that deep inside of him he loved only me.

"Graduation night from high school, he told me that he and his family were moving to another state and that he would come back to get me. I waited for five years in that small town, thinking he would return. He didn't come back. When I moved to California, I met my ex-husband. When we went to a doctors' convention, we flew on the plane that Carl was flying. I finally saw him after many years.

"With questions and with research, I found out about you, Michelle, Cliff and Summer. I know that Carl still loves me. His kids are *my* kids and not yours. With you dead, Carl will feel so stricken with grief that he will come back to me again!"

Molly's eyes were completely crazy, so I did the only thing I knew to do and say. Her mental stability was no longer there.

"Molly, I hear your son, Cliff, calling for you. He needs his mommy. Go to him, as there is something wrong with him!"

When I said this, Molly let go of my arms and stood up straight, holding the knife. I yanked the covers from around me and climbed out of bed as quickly as I could.

Molly turned around and faced me with the knife held high. She was getting ready to stab me when I grabbed her hand to keep this from happening.

Michelle had awakened and heard a noise in my bedroom. She started down the hallway to see what the noise was. When she opened the door, she could see that I was in danger. She quietly walked to the night stand and pulled out Carl's pistol that she knew was loaded.

By then, Molly and I were standing in front of the bedroom window that was open. Molly was trying desperately to get my hand off of the knife when Michelle raised the pistol to shoot Molly in the back. Molly, seeing that I wasn't going to stop fighting and that I was standing in front of an open window two stories up, kept pushing me closer to it.

When Michelle saw this, she screamed, "Molly, *stop!*" and held the gun, ready to shoot her in the back.

Molly turned around and Michelle fired. She shot Molly in the chest and heart. As Molly fell backwards, we both went out the bedroom window.

My head hit the cement sidewalk and Molly was dead before she hit the ground.

Carl had entered the house and came running up

the stairs. He had heard his gun fire. Cliff woke up and also was running down the hall. Summer was awake and crying in her crib.

The neighbors across from us had seen the commotion and called the police. With them came the ambulance. For Molly came the car from the morgue.

So again, here I have lain, for probably many days, in my hospital room, in a bed with my family around me, day and night.

I hear Carl speaking to me. "Carla, I am so sorry again. I had no idea I was putting you in danger. I should have listened to you and heard your words instead of letting my own way of thinking take over. Please wake up, so I can show you the deep love again that I have in my heart for you," Carl said with tears streaming down his face.

At last I awoke and I looked into his eyes. I could see him and I did survive. I had beat the odds the doctors had given me to live.

With the love of my family, I knew I would make it. I was even able to speak. I told Carl what Molly had told me and what she had done to us.

Then I said with a smile on my face, "Were there any more hearts that you broke when you were younger?"

Carl laughed and said, "No, Carla, you are and always will be my only love."

PART 3

Spring Break

— 1 —
The Journey

I feel that I haven't ever been good with introductions, especially when it comes to explaining things to people about either myself or my line of work.

A company based in Chicago by the name of Calaburt is where I have been employed for many years. They, unlike myself, believe in my ability to promote and sell a line of women's clothing that I design. The clothing line I am referring to is what I named *Spring Break.* Calaburt not only promotes my line—like me—to major department stores all over the world, but also many chains across the nation. I employ sophisticated marketing techniques to sell *Spring Break.*

In order to elevate my clothing line, I travel to different locations to promote sales for Calaburt. Whether I choose to drive or fly, I take a variety of samples to identify the quality of each garment from *Spring Break*, to show a complete design that will be distributed to them.

Also, I furnish to each chain of the many department stores a catalog of my clothing line with a removable updated one-page sheet that shows them in detail the wholesale cost and the retail pricing that the many stores can choose and order from.

At times, I have picked a town or city where I can easily host a fashion show. Also in the fashion industry, I attend different trade shows where I display *Spring Break*.

My name is Mike Fargo. Today I am leaving to travel to Abilene, Texas, with several samples of *Spring Break* to promote and sell to another big company. I have been penciled in to also do a couple of fashion shows along the way. Calaburt has me traveling more than I am here in the windy city of Chicago.

Today, as I am just about out of the city, I am stuck in traffic. I have turned on the radio to see what the highways are like, not knowing whether I should take the interstate or country roads when I have reached the ones that I am familiar with.

My intent is to arrive at my scheduled stops, making sure that I arrive on time. With the radio telling me that there is a lot of highway under construction, in order for me to avoid a bunch of unnecessary problems for myself, I need to take the old highways. Some I have been on before, and some will be new to me. I can see construction signs ahead, so it is time to take my *Spring Break* van toward the exits going south.

When I rounded the exit, as far as I could see, the highway would be clear sailing for me the whole way, until I needed to make another turn on a different highway leading south. Unfortunately, if the truth be known, there would be joy about to happen in my life, but I also would experience something very terrifying that I would never imagine happening to me.

I had driven on a highway which led me to turn onto an unfamiliar highway, which I already knew I was going to encounter along the way.

Up ahead, I could see what appeared to be a person walking with a suitcase. When I stopped to offer a ride, I could see that this person was a woman.

"Do you want a ride?" I asked.

"Yes, and thank you. I have been walking for hours," she said as she slid open the connecting door to load her heavy suitcase.

As the woman climbed into the front seat, I asked, "Where are you headed?"

"Anywhere but around here," she replied in a soft voice.

"Well, I am going to Abilene, Texas, with several stops in between. If you would like to ride along with me, I will let you out at any stop where you want to get out."

"Again, thank you. By the way, my name is Lori," she said as she smiled and reached over to shake my hand.

"Okay, Lori. Abilene bound we are headed. And my name is Mike."

I had driven for hours and the sun was starting to set, and before long it would be dark. It had been a while since either one of us had said a word. I could see that Lori was in deep thought about something.

"If you don't mind me asking, why were you walking with a heavy suitcase?" I asked.

Without hesitation and giving my question any thought of denial, she said, "Tomorrow was supposed to be my wedding day. My fiancé and I were headed to a small town to get married by the Justice of the Peace. The more we talked, while we were driving, the more I found out about what he had been doing on his last business trip that he had just come back from.

"Apparently he ran into his old girlfriend, Sandra.

He tried to explain to me that he had no feelings for her any longer, and that he didn't know that she would be in Marco when he arrived there.

"I wanted to believe him, but when we were checking into the motel, my fiancé had left his wallet in the glove compartment. When he went out to the car to get it, the night clerk asked me to go ahead and sign the guest registry for us.

"As I was looking down it to sign in, I noticed where my fiancé and Sandra had signed their names for five different nights. That was the length of time that he was gone. He had been sleeping with her every night, sneaking away from her just long enough to call me.

"When he came back into the motel to pay and show his ID, I told him what I had seen. He kept saying that nothing had happened between them, but after he kept repeating himself for the third time, I slapped him and told him I didn't want to ever see his face around me again.

"I grabbed my suitcase that was sitting on the floor and walked out the front door. When I got outside, I took my engagement ring and threw it as far as I could throw.

"My parents tried to tell me that he was not good enough for me, but I wouldn't listen. I thought that they were just wanting me to stay around home and not have a life of my own.

"So I hid to wait for him to leave, and then I went into the motel myself to register for the night. I have been hitchhiking ever since," Lori said with still a soft voice that sounded tired and full of sadness.

"I'm sorry, Lori. I had something similar happen to me years ago. I had worked my way through a university, struggling to drive back and forth to my hometown, to make sure that I spent as much time with my girlfriend as my job and school would allow. We had dated for a couple of years and I wanted to believe that she was as much in love with me as I was with her.

"One day, I chose to call work and make the excuse that I was sick, and with that, decided to skip some classes that day. When I arrived home, I found a note on the kitchen table telling me that she had decided to leave me, and go live in a different town with an old boyfriend.

"My trust in women and relationships ended with me staying single ever since," I said as I turned my head to look at Lori. Finding her asleep let me know that she was exhausted from walking and hitchhiking for many miles.

The next town we came to, I drove into the parking lot of a motel. After going inside and registering, I went back to get Lori. I picked her up to carry her from the front seat of the *Spring Break* van. When we entered the room, with her head leaning against mine and her still being sound asleep, I laid her down on one of the beds to sleep comfortably for the night.

As I was laying her down, her cap that she had been wearing fell off her head onto the floor. I could see that she was very beautiful with long, flowing dark hair.

I turned out the lamp next to her bed and went over to my bed to sleep. It had been a long drive that day.

— 2 —

Talent and Charm

I had already made coffee the next morning and was sitting at the small table in the room when Lori woke up. She opened her eyes, looked around the room, and saw me.

"Mike, I don't remember walking in here," she said.

"I know you don't, as you fell asleep in the van. It was late and I knew it was time to stop for the night. We were both tired. I didn't want to wake you up, so I carried you to this room, where we both could get a good night of rest."

"Thank you for helping me, Mike, you are a decent man," she responded with her soft voice that still sounded way too sad.

"Like I told you, my destination is Abilene, before I return to Chicago. If you want, you can come along with me for the complete ride, or I am willing to double back and take you home."

"I have no home, Mike. When I left my hometown, I left there for good. I will go with you to Abilene, and then you can let me out there."

"That works for me, Lori," I replied.

I could see that she needed help and I wasn't going to just drop her off in the middle of nowhere. If I only knew now what was waiting for us up ahead, and would find out later, I would have left her at the motel. Then again, I would have missed out on so much joy as well.

After sitting across from Lori and seeing her smile and laugh, I knew that I had done the right thing by stopping to pick her up.

Soon after, we were on our way, driving again to a small city, where I was going to show different pieces of fabric along with designs that I had created for *Spring Break*. Seeing Lori finally looking happy was a pleasant sight. I didn't know her history in her life, but was sure that she needed a friend to talk to.

At the small city, I had scheduled a fashion show where models would be wearing the fashions that I had created. Lori was tall, slender and very beautiful, so I decided to ask her if she would like to take part in my show.

"Lori, as you know, I am a fashion designer who created my own clothing line. Today we are stopping at a company that I do business with. I will be hosting a fashion show there. Would you like to earn some money modeling for it?" I asked.

"Yes, Mike, I would be happy to help you out. You don't need to pay me, as you already have done so much for me," Lori replied again with a smile on her face.

As we drove down the highway, laughing, we talked like we had known each other for years and about so many different things. We stopped at a place to eat once we had arrived at the city where I needed to be.

Lori helped me take in what I had brought to promote for *Spring Break*.

When I went into an office room to show to the CEO of the company what I had brought with me, Lori was in a room with the other models, preparing for her walk down the runway.

When I was finished, I found her. I could not believe my eyes. She looked exquisite. All I could do was smile at her as she did back at me. I felt this was one of the biggest things that had happened to her in her entire life.

I walked out on the stage and started my introduction to the show. I then brought out actual models to give Lori a chance to breathe before she walked out. To my amazement, when she did, she walked out like she owned the stage. She was not only very beautiful, but very talented as well. I had two more shows to do before we reached Abilene, and if she agreed, I was going to include her in every show I did, unless she felt the need to be on her own again.

When all the models were standing on the stage after the show, I called Lori to my side and thanked everyone for coming. Lori held my hand and smiled at everyone. Her glow was very noticeable and it had been one of my most productive shows that I'd ever had.

As Lori changed back into her clothes, I waited for her. When we ran down the steps and to the van, I said, "Lori, you were amazing in there!"

"Thanks, Mike," she replied.

We got in the van and as we drove away, I took her to a place that I knew of there in that city that was elegant. We walked through the front door of the restaurant with her wearing the black dress that I had designed. I also gave her jewelry to wear with it.

People were staring at us like we were royalty. As we walked across the floor to our assigned table, people still continued to stare. The way Lori walked, talked and acted made me wonder just where she had actually come from.

When we sat down to review the menu and wine

list, I had to ask her a question.

"Lori, today on the runway you carried yourself in the manner of a professional model. Have you ever done any modeling before now?"

"No, Mike, I haven't done it before. I am the daughter of a very well-respected, rich family. I have attended many formal occasions and was taught by a nanny how to glow in the eyes of the public. This is why I can't go back home. My mother and father told me that my ex-fiancé was not good enough for me, and because I refused to listen, I don't want to go back there as I feel like a disappointment to them."

"Lori, I don't know your family, but the short time we have known each other, I can tell that you have never, or would never, be a disappointment to anyone."

This again put a smile on her face. In a couple of days, we had become very good friends. Lori was not only beautiful, sweet, intelligent and alluring, she had a sensitive side to her which reminded me that money and fame aren't everything in life. They don't buy complete happiness. This was something that I had, over the years, put in the back of my mind.

When we left the motel the next morning, we laughed and sang songs with the radio blaring. With Lori's help, she had taught me how to enjoy life and how to be meek again.

We had turned off on another road that would take us to the destination where we needed to be. I had an appointment with a different CEO to again show fabric and designs. *Spring Break* had been on the market for years and was high in demand. The models that this company furnished for my show were awesome, but there was no comparison to Lori as she walked out on the runway again.

After the show, I would be asking her if she would

model for me in Chicago. If the answer was yes she would be riding back with me.

Later, as we were driving away, I said, "Lori, you did a great job again today. I would like to hire you as a full-time model for Calaburt and for me. You would be living in Chicago and at times traveling with me when I leave the city to promote *Spring Break* in a different part of the country, or the world. What do you think? Are you interested?"

"Yes again, Mike. I do need a full-time job. I promise you that I won't let you down," she replied.

"Great," I said as I put my hand out to shake hers. This was my way of saying, "Welcome on board, Lori." She knew what I was doing and just smiled back at me.

Tomorrow would mean a longer day of traveling, and tonight another night out on the town, to celebrate my new model, Lori.

When the sun came up the next morning, we were on our way to Abilene. We had made several turns onto an old road that I was not familiar with. The road I had taken before was blocked off. I wasn't sure where it would take us, or even where we were at. I just knew that we had to be at the biggest fashion show in the morning.

I was feeling unsettled in my mind, hoping that I could find a side road that would connect us back onto the main highway that would take us to where we needed to be.

"Lori, we are lost in unfamiliar territory. Hopefully, we won't be for much longer."

"Okay, Mike. I'm not worried," she said.

We continued to drive for hours, and up ahead we saw three men standing next to an old truck that appeared to be broken down. We were a long ways from a town and I needed to stop and help them.

When we pulled over to the side of the road, I climbed out of the van to talk to them. "It looks like you are broke down."

"Yes, it appears to be that way. This old truck was on its last leg," an older man said.

"Are we close to a town?" I asked.

"No, we are quite a ways away from any town. Now we are stranded here. This old truck quit working."

"I have room in my van, if you would like to climb in. I can take you to the next town," I said.

"Yes, if you don't mind, that would help us."

"Sure, no problem," I told the older man as we walked back to the van. Now, instead of having just Lori with me, I had three men as well. Time was running out and I needed to find the connecting highway to get us back on track, so that we could do the last show.

"Are you familiar with this area?" I asked.

"No, we are going to Abilene to a stock show. That road block that was set up had us turning onto *this* road, as apparently it did you as well."

"Yes, it did the same thing to us. My name is Mike, and this is Lori," I said.

"Pleased to meet you. My name is Harry," the older man said as he reached out to shake our hands.

The other two men extended their hands and shook hands with us as well.

"Hello, I'm Pete, and this is Ray," Pete said.

"None of us are from around here. What leads you to these parts of Texas?" Pete asked.

"I'm a fashion designer from a women's clothing line called *Spring Break*. You probably saw that name on the van when you were getting in. Lori is my top model. We were on our way to Abilene to do a fashion show scheduled for tomorrow.

"This is the first time I have been on this road, and have no clue where we are going now, " I replied.

"Where did you come from?" Ray asked.

"Chicago," I answered. I didn't want to speak for Lori as I wasn't sure she wanted them to know, so I had both of us based living in Chicago. This answer seemed to pacify all three men.

"Where are *you* from?" I asked.

"Wichita Falls, Texas is where we are from," Harry said.

We had driven for hours and I felt like we were going in circles. Up ahead, for the first time on the old road, I saw a light on. Maybe they could help us find the exit off of this road, and find the highway that we needed to be on.

The closer we got, the more that I could see that we were driving to a building that resembled a rundown café. If it was a place where we could eat, hopefully they had a couple of spare rooms to camp out in until morning. Maybe they might even know of a shortcut out of here.

As we drove up to the building, I stopped and announced that I would go to the door, to see if they were open, and to check things out. I could see that Lori was tired and we needed a place to stop for the night.

"Do you want me to go with you?" Harry asked.

"No, I will be fine, Harry, but thanks."

"You never know what you might encounter, Mike. You are in Texas now," Harry said as he laughed.

I laughed as well and wondered, as I walked to the front door, if I would have a gun pointed at me from the other side of the door when it opened.

Standing at the door, knocking, I was ready to turn around and walk away, when a lady opened the door.

"Well, for Pete's sake, the door was unlocked. You should have just walked in," she said.

"I'm not from here, and honestly, I didn't know what to do," I replied.

"Well, come on in. You can see we are open for business," she commented as she turned and walked toward the counter.

I could see that it was an old café that still was in business. I motioned for Lori, Harry, Pete and Ray to come in, and then I closed the door.

"How many are there of you?" the woman asked.

Before I had time to answer, Lori and the others had come in and sat down at a table.

The lady asked if we wanted coffee and I told her yes. When she returned with five cups and a pot of coffee, I asked, "How far are we from the main high-way?"

"You are about a half a day away from Abilene."

I knew then that we weren't going to make it there in time for Lori and I to take care of the fashion show.

"I have a very important business meeting tomorrow, and I need to use your phone to call them, if I can," I asked.

"Oh, we are too far out for phone service," she replied.

In my mind I wondered why this café was still in existence. It was way off the beaten path of any high-way in the area. How could they afford to keep it open?

"Do you get much business here?" I asked.

"We get what we can handle."

The lady poured the coffee and, knowing that by the time we reached Abilene it would be too late to do the show, I asked, "Do you have a couple of spare rooms we can rent from you for the night?" I could see that

Lori, Harry, Pete and Ray wanted to call it a day, as I did.

"We will find a place to put all of you," she replied.

At the time, I felt uncomfortable about the café and the woman, but could see that we were there for the night.

— 3 —

Drugged

The more coffee we drank, the sleepier we all were getting. With my eyes open, it looked like the room was spinning and I could see that Harry had fallen asleep sitting up in his chair. Pete had fallen off his chair and was lying on the floor. Lori and Ray had their heads resting on the table.

As the room continued to spin, I could see and hear the woman laughing at us in an evil voice. All I could say was, "You drugged us."

When I woke up, I saw Lori lying next to me on a basement floor. The cement was cold and hard. There were no windows to climb out of, but a slight amount of sunlight was coming through the old cement blocks. We could barely see. The door was thick and I could smell an odor of what appeared to be blood.

Harry, Pete and Ray were not with us. I wanted to scream out for help, but knew that this place was too far away from anyone or anything, and no one would be able to hear us.

Soon Lori opened her eyes and sat up abruptly. When she saw me, she said, "Mike, what are we doing in here?"

"I'm not sure, Lori, other than we are in what I believe to be the basement of the café."

"I don't remember much after we sat down at the

table and started drinking coffee," she replied.

"The room looked like it was spinning, and I could see that all of you were asleep. The last thing I remember seeing was that woman laughing at us in an evil voice. I told her that she had drugged us."

"Where is Harry, Pete and Ray?" Lori asked.

"I don't know, Lori! They must be in another room. I just know that we need to find a way out of here."

Lori agreed with me, and we sat there, waiting for someone to come and check on us.

After a couple of hours, we could hear talking.

"When the other fresh meat is taken care of, moron," the crazy lady from the café said as we could hear the hit to the back of the head of the man that appeared to be her son. "Go tell your brother to take care of that van outside. We don't need anyone seeing it and coming in here, asking about it."

I knew that here would be the last place anyone would look for us. Also, where were they going to take us from here? I could see that Lori was very frightened as she was shaking and scooting closer and closer to me. I put my arm around her and said, "Don't be afraid, Lori. I won't let anything happen to you."

"I know, Mike. I just wish I knew why they put us down here and what they plan to do with us."

"Me, too, Lori. Me too."

Sitting there with questions, we heard screaming from a man, saying, "Please, please don't hurt me! Please stop!"

The voice was not that of Harry, Pete or Ray. Someone else was at the mercy of these crazy people, besides us.

Because of the road being blocked off, it was hard to say how many people were down here, and in a different room, waiting for these people. The odor of blood was very strong. I was so terrified. No matter what, I wouldn't let Lori see my fear. I continued to hold her.

We heard a steel cart or table coming past the room. We were in trouble if they were coming to get us. We were in danger and I had to figure out how to get us out of here alive.

Lori kept telling me she was hungry and scared. I told her I was also hungry, and I reassured her that she shouldn't be afraid. I would protect her from anything.

We heard more screaming and begging, coming this time from a woman. There was a noise that sounded like an ax hitting the steel table, and the screaming stopped. The comment about needing fresh meat made me wonder if the woman and her sons were cannibals that were killing people for fresh meat and the flesh from their bones. All we could do was wait it out until someone came through the door to get us.

We heard people walking around outside and pushing tables and carts around for hours. I was still wondering what happened to Harry, Pete and Ray. My question was, were they still alive or were they screaming somewhere that we couldn't hear them?

Finally, the noise stopped. We both were shaking from the terror that surrounded us. Lori and I could see the sunshine coming through the cracks of the cement blocks starting to fade.

I knew that I had missed my last fashion show in Texas that day, and that Calaburt would be notified of my *no show*. The only thing they didn't know about was *where* I was. All I could do was pray that a search helicopter from the air would find my van, and someone would rescue us in time.

Or would these crazy people come get us tonight, to take us to where the other victims met their doom?

Lori slept close to me that night, in my arms. Soon I drifted off to sleep as well. We were both sitting ducks awaiting our demise. Had our fate been decided for us?

— 4 —
Waiting

As the night progressed, I kept waking up every time I heard any kind of a noise. If I could be, I wanted to be as alert as possible, in case someone came through the door. Maybe I could get to them before they got to me. This was my plan as I continued to hold Lori.

Like before, we woke up with a slight amount of light, with people talking outside the door.

"No, I did move that van. I hooked onto it with the tractor and took it down the road about a mile. I put it where the other cars are." A different son of the crazy woman had spoken.

"You are stupid! Not everyone breaks down in the same spot! Go back out there and don't come back in here until you have done it right this time!" the crazy lady said in anger.

Then we heard, "Ma, do I need to go take down the barrier that is blocking the highway, or do we not have enough fresh meat yet?" It was another voice coming from someone we hadn't heard before.

"No, you idiot, leave the barrier alone!" was again spoken by the crazy woman.

All of this made me wonder how many I would need to fight to get Lori and myself safely out of here. Why were they killing people? Lori and I were enclosed in a nut house, held captive by these crazy people that had to have fresh meat. Once again, I asked myself, "Are they cannibals?"

It wasn't very long and we heard another person screaming for help, and then what sounded like an ax hitting a steel table. The screaming had stopped. Within a short time thereafter, we would hear the table passing by the room we were locked in. It was like being locked in a cold, dark meat locker with nowhere to run and nowhere to hide.

Since I was convinced that it wouldn't be long before Lori and I would be next, I had to come up with a real plan that I was sure of that would take Lori and me out of here to a safe place.

Talking softly to Lori as I didn't want to startle her, I said, "Lori, I have a plan, and it is the only one I can come up with. Not knowing how many men are going to come in here, we need to be prepared for anything and everything. My guess is that they will have one person waiting outside the door, in case one of us would try to escape.

"I have been listening to all of them talking. One of the men has left to dispose of all the cars that he had parked in the same location. If I don't hear any new voices, that leaves the crazy woman that they all call Ma, and two other men. Regardless, when I start to hear voices of them unlocking our door, I am going to stand behind the door. When it opens, I want you to quietly move to the right side of the room, where it is darker, away from the light that slightly comes through the cement blocks.

"It is dark enough in here that when he does come into this room, he won't see me, or you, and if I'm right, he will be looking around the room for both of us. When he turns and sees you, I will step behind him to grab him from the back, where I will snap his neck. When the other man hears him fall to the floor, he will come into the room to see what the noise is.

"I am thinking that he will be the one carrying the ax or a knife. I haven't heard a gun fire, so I don't think they are killing their victims like that. When he comes through the door, I want you to start running out of here as fast as you can. I will jump him from behind.

"As much as I have heard from this room, I believe the stairs that lead from the first floor to here are straight across the hall from us. When you get up the stairs, I want you running, after you open the door. If, by chance, that crazy woman is up there and tries to hold onto you, there is an iron paper holder on the left side of the counter. I want you to grab it and hit her as hard as you can in the head.

"After that, Lori, I don't want you to come back looking for me. I will find you outside after you have hidden. When the third man that is outside moving the cars around on the road comes back inside, I want you to run down the road as if we were still driving in the same direction, to find the highway until you find the van.

"They took everything out of my pockets, but I do have a hidden key below the left corner on the bumper. I want you to drive out of here and into the nearest town, to tell the Sheriff everything, so no one else goes through this. Do you understand, Lori?" I asked.

"Yes, Mike, I do," Lori replied with a tear falling from her eye.

"As for Harry, Pete and Ray, I am afraid they already have become fresh meat."

Lori agreed, and now it was time to wait it out.

We sat for hours, waiting, and finally the time had come. Once again I heard talking outside the door.

We heard this:

"Ma! Is it time yet?"

"It's time, and you better not screw it up," the crazy woman said.

"Why would I screw it up, Ma?"

"Because one of your other brothers is outside moving cars around that he screwed up on, and your other brother is in there, waiting for you to take them to the room," she said as she pointed at a room that reeked from the odor of fresh blood.

"Can I have my way with her first, Ma? She smells so good. I licked her neck when I carried her down here, and she tastes so good. Can I, Ma? Can I? Can I keep her?"

I could tell that this might be easier than I thought, as this guy didn't sound too bright.

"No, you cannot do that! You don't do well with any pet, you idiot! I'm going upstairs to prepare for more fresh meat." With her finger in his face, the crazy woman once more said, "Don't screw it up!"

I felt like this might be easier than Lori and I could possibly expect it to be.

The man waited for his mother to walk up the stairs and leave the basement. He was going to take me first to his brother, and then come back to Lori, to have his way with her before he took her to the room. The trap was set as I stood behind the door, waiting for him to enter. Lori had moved away from the small amount of light that was still barely shining in.

When the door opened, the man was looking into a semi-dark room for us. He was carrying an ax.

As he spotted Lori, he had forgotten about me. Lori had unbuttoned her shirt and all he could see was her soft pale skin with a black bra showing. Lori had a plan of her own.

The man stood there, staring, smiling, and then stepped forward, saying, "Oh, baby!" He had forgotten about me.

At that time, I came quietly around the door and, with my hands, I snapped his neck. He and his ax fell to the floor. Lori and I thought we were free as we started for the door. But the other brother had come out of the room to see what was taking so long.

When he rounded the corner of the room and saw his little brother lying on the floor, dead, he grew angry and came at me with the ax he was carrying. He was taller and stronger than his little brother, and I grabbed his right arm to keep him from striking me with the blade of the ax.

I was weak and tired from hunger and lack of sleep. He knocked me to the floor.

Lori picked up the ax from the younger brother that lay dead, and as hard as she could, raised it above her head. With a downward motion, she stabbed it in the middle of his back. He raised up some and then fell over. He, too, was dead.

I stood up and told Lori to run up the stairs. I would be right behind her.

When we went through the upstairs door, the crazy lady saw us and started for the front door, screaming for her sons to come get us. She was wasting her breath, as the two of them that were in there lay dead in the basement.

As she reached the door to lock it, I smashed her head in with the large iron paper holder. She was where she belonged. She was no longer in this lifetime, and had to justify her actions now to God, who saved our lives.

I opened the door slowly to look outside for the third time. He would be making his appearance soon, and now was not the time for us to make any mistakes. It was getting dark, which was what we needed to happen.

There was no one in sight, so we ran out of the building to a mass of trees across the road. We waited there until we saw the third son walk up the steps and into what Lori and I named The Slaughter House.

We started running again in the direction he had come from. We had to reach the van and get out of there fast.

It seemed like we had run a couple of miles when we found my *Spring Break* van not far from the other cars that were stashed amongst the trees. I went to the front bumper, found the hidden key, started the van, and Lori and I drove straight ahead in hopes of finding the connecting highway.

I grabbed Lori's hand and said, "After all of that, do you still want to hang with me?"

"There's no one on Earth I would rather be with, Mike."

We continued to drive until we found the highway and a town. I told the Sheriff about everything we had endured the last few days. He sent a helicopter, loaded with men, to find the remaining son of the crazy woman. Also, to see if Harry, Pete and Ray were still alive.

After we ate and waited for the return of the men in the helicopter, Lori laid her head on my shoulder to sleep. She felt safe and protected being with me. I, too, felt this way, as if she would have followed my plan in the basement and ran instead of staying behind to stab the second man in the back. I wouldn't have been alive to help us both survive.

When morning came, we were awakened by the sound of the helicopter landing. We both got up from the chair and walked to the door. All the men were climbing out.

The Sheriff walked out to meet them and talk. I thought everyone had unloaded. Then I saw two men hanging onto the third man that I hadn't killed. Also, to our surprise, coming off the helicopter last were Harry, Pete and Ray. They, too, had managed to stay alive.

Lori and I ran as fast as we could to greet them.

"We thought that you were dead too. We heard a woman scream … and men."

"Man, were we happy to get rescued from that nut house," Harry said.

"How did you get out of there?" Pete asked.

"Well, let's just say that a determined, beautiful lady by the name of Lori had a better plan than I did," I said as I pulled Lori close to me.

With more laughing and talking, all five of us, with our arms around each other, were so thankful to be alive and walked away.

— 5 —

Knowing the Facts

Harry, Pete and Ray went on to Abilene to attend what they could at the stock show. Lori and I chose to come back to Chicago, where I introduced her to everyone as my new top model.

A few days after we returned, I got a call from the Sheriff, telling me that they had flushed out The Slaughter House. From the bones of many people, they had discovered many who had been reported as missing for several years.

Also, the cars that were hidden had been removed and the barrier on that dirt road was destroyed.

He also told me that they had found a big freezer full of packaged meat that had been tested. It all came from human flesh and bones.

The Sheriff also said that the man who was brought in confessed to many killings and that for years the packages of human flesh and meat were used in the café until the interstate was put in.

No one went past the old café again. This drove the woman crazy and she didn't want to leave there, so she researched and found someone that would buy meat from her. The place she had been selling to had no idea what kind of meat it was.

Knowing all of this, and the fact that we believed that the people were cannibals in the beginning, was a very good reason why Lori and I chose from that moment on to only eat fish and white meat.

Lori and I were scheduled in for another road trip, in a different direction this time. If it wasn't for *Spring Break*, I wouldn't have ever met her.

My clothing line was not only a success, but I had found myself again.

I know that all of you are wondering what happened between Lori and myself when we returned to Chicago.

That night when I went to bed, I reached over and turned off my lamp. Lori climbed in bed, turning off her lamp as she snuggled close against me. "Good night, husband."

"Good night, my wife."

PART 4

The Cabin at the End
of the Road

— 1 —
The Move

It was the summer of 1980. Most of us wore feathered hair, side ponytails, miniskirts, off-the-shoulder shirts and my favorite, Levi jeans. When my pants wore out, I placed different patches all over them.

That day I had come back to my house, happier than I had been in years. For some people, what I did that day when I went to the company manager I worked for, might have been harder for them than it was for me. What I had done was a blessing. I quit my job of twenty years.

I was getting older and wanted to travel and live in a place where I felt serene and joy, instead of always the hustle and bustle of constant traffic from the city. I'm not saying that living in a city is totally the worst place to live, but as I get older, I realize that if I don't make a move now, there is a good chance I won't.

Having saved some money over the course of twenty years, I knew I would be fine if it took me a while to find a job.

My name is Peggy Stern. I had just gone outside with the Realtor to talk to her as she placed the *For Sale* sign on my front lawn. It was just one of those last-minute things to take care of before piling my luggage in the back of my car.

My destination was Fremont, Wyoming. I had rented a cabin to live in until my house sold. My plans were to pick up two of my closest friends along the way, for a couple weeks of fun and girl talk. This visit with them could be the last one for a while.

When the sun came up, I was out the door of my house and waving to my neighbor across the street, who was standing outside in his yard, getting ready to walk his dog.

As usual, the traffic was horrible and backed up with everyone leaving the city at the same time.

I was looking forward to driving my two friends to the cabin. We were very excited and it was going to be a good vacation for them, staying with me in the cabin until their return home. We wanted it to be a vacation that they wouldn't forget. This is a statement that soon would hold true for the rest of our lives.

Driving in the direction of Wyoming, I saw a young woman walking. I stopped to pick her up. She was quiet after asking me to let her off at a certain place five miles down the highway.

She didn't look like she went outside much as she was pale in color. Her dress was light blue and maybe something her grandmother had picked out for her to wear. It was outdated and something long ago that had been worn to a dance.

Just barely before I got to the spot where she wanted to be let out, the girl told me that I could stop up ahead. I pulled over to the side of the road and she opened the door to climb out.

With her, she had brought a light blue rose that she had hung onto. When she left the car, she left the rose on the seat.

I felt sad for her because she looked very poor, and I thought the rose was something that meant a lot to her. I turned the car around to give her back her flower. When I got to the exact spot where I had dropped her off, I saw a graveyard.

I got out of the car and walked into it. I thought maybe I would see her walking and could call out for her to stop. I saw nothing but a picture of the girl dating back to 1912. This was the date on her tombstone. I laid the flower on the ground in front of it and stood there long enough to watch it turn black.

I ran back to my car and continued to drive out and away from there. I had heard of such happenings with hitchhikers that disappeared, but didn't want to believe that this would happen to me.

When I reached the next town, where I chose to spend the night, I happened to bring it up to the desk clerk about how I had stopped for a young girl who wanted a ride and ended up with her picture on a tombstone. Also the flower turning black.

I was told that this was the same girl that walks up and down the highway, and that there was a myth about her. The myth stated that if the person didn't stop to pick her up, that person would forever have bad luck.

With all of this being told to me, I was scared and hoping that I didn't come across another hitchhiker again. It was a very quiet night for me. I needed the rest that I got.

The next uneventful day of driving, I was going to be on time picking up my friend, Betty Pierce. It had been quite a while since I had seen Betty. We had talked on the phone, written letters and sent cards, but hadn't spent time together since high school.

After a couple of hours, I was looking on a paper that had directions to Betty's home. Before long, Betty, Kathy and I would be together again. They both were going to fly home after all of our fun at the cabin was over, within a couple of weeks.

Betty heard my car pull up close to her home and she was headed out the door, walking toward me with a huge smile.

After she threw her bag into the back seat, she climbed in. "You made exceptional time. It is so good to see you."

"I know. I had a scary thing happen to me on the highway between here and Washington. I saw a young woman walking. It was starting to get dark, so I picked her up. She looked like she was needing a ride. When I went to let her out of the car, she left a light blue rose on the seat. I turned around to find her, to give it back to her. When I returned to the spot where I had dropped her off, she was nowhere in sight.

"So I pulled the car over and went to find her. As I kept walking, I reached a graveyard and the tombstone that showed an old photograph of her on it. She was wearing the same old dress that she had on that night. I laid the light blue rose down on the grass where she was buried, and I stood there long enough to watch it turn black. My thought after that was to run to my car and leave fast.

"A night clerk told me that she walks the highway a lot before dark. The myth is that if a person doesn't stop and pick her up, that person will have bad luck brought to them the rest of their life. I am so happy that I picked her up," I said as I wiped away sweat beads on my face.

"Oh my, Peggy, that would have scared me to death."

"It almost did, Betty. It almost did," I said as we drove away.

— 2 —

The Oil Truck

"I am so excited. We are going to have so much fun!"

"Things could get very interesting all right, Betty," I replied.

The next scheduled stop was in a town not far from there, where our other friend, Kathy and her family, lived. Betty and I talked for hours, and again about high school.

As we got closer to Kathy's hometown, driving on an interstate headed east, there was a huge oil truck that kept riding my back bumper. It wouldn't back off and both of us were starting to get very nervous. There was the other lane, where it could pass us, but the man who was driving it kept sounding the horn as if he wanted me to move over, so he could pass me. I would move to the other lane and he would too, still continuing to drive up close to the rear of my car. There was no way I could get away from him.

"Peggy, what is that man doing?" Betty asked.

"I don't know, Betty. I just know that I can't slow down to pull over or stop, as he will cause us to wreck. I am going as fast as I can now, to try to get away from him, so that I can pull over. Up ahead, there is a steep grade and I think I can lose him there, as he won't be able to go as fast as us."

As we got closer to the grade, I floored the pedal. Not knowing if there were dangerous curves up ahead, I just wanted the truck far enough behind me, in order to make an escape away from it.

As my car drove up the hill, the truck slightly started to slow down. I was sure that I had the upper hand on it, and by the time I got to the top of the hill and had started down, the truck wouldn't be able to see us or catch us.

Just before I started down the curvy hill, I looked in my mirror, to see if the truck was anywhere in sight. I couldn't see it, so I was convinced that we had outrun it.

Wiping the sweat off of our faces, we were both sure that we were safe now.

"Betty, I think we did it. I don't see the truck. Now I think we can breathe."

"I hope you are right, Peggy," Betty replied.

Unfortunately, when we got too comfortable in the fact that we had lost the out-of-control truck and driver, I could see him rolling up on us again at a high-ball speed. I, at that time, had no place to pull the car over, so he could drive past us. So I, too, increased my speed. I was going to outrun him, no matter what it took.

I kept switching lanes back and forth, telling him in my way to just pass me. He would switch lanes when I did and when I would return back to the other lane, he would continue to sound his loud horn and still try to ride my bumper.

"Peggy, I am really scared!" Betty said.

"Me too, Betty, but at this point I have no choice but to keep driving like this, until he passes us."

I had increased my speed by 20 miles per hour and was flying down the interstate with him hugging my car bumper. I drove like this for quite a while and kept checking the mirror, to see where he was next. When I looked again just a second after I had checked before, the truck had disappeared. This was not possible. It hadn't passed us, but now it was nowhere in sight!

"Betty, did you see where that truck went?" I asked as she, too, had been watching her side mirror.

"No, it just disappeared! I just looked and it was behind us, and now it is totally missing," Betty replied with an excitable voice.

"I have been watching too, and what the heck is going on?"

"I don't know, but I'm afraid that it will find us again!"

"When we get to the next town, even if it is behind us again, it will have to slow down long enough for us to leave the interstate," I replied with a shocked, but relieved look on my face.

We continued to watch for more hours and there was no sign of the big truck that had been tailgating us. There was an exit ramp up ahead that looked like a truck stop. I wanted to stop there for coffee and to report the driver. If he did stop there, I wanted him to be in trouble for trying to kill us.

When we walked through the café, we walked up to the counter where I saw a state trooper sitting. "Excuse me, sir, I want to report an oil tank truck driver that was trying to kill my friend and me. He was trying to run us off the interstate as he wouldn't quit tailgating me. I had to drive faster to keep my friend and me alive. Just before we pulled in here, he was behind us one second, and then the next second the oil truck disappeared."

"I'm sorry that you and your friend had to endure that experience. This same thing has happened to many people on this interstate. It is the same story every time someone else tells it, and all I can tell you is the same thing I have told others. You, too, were followed by a ghost truck. For some unknown reason, it always appears every day at around the same time. There is no driver. Just the truck."

At that time, Betty and I had both turned white. Between the young girl that was a ghost walking on the highway, hitchhiking, and the ghost truck that could have killed us, I couldn't wait to get to the cabin.

We thanked the state trooper for his reply to us on what we had seen and been followed by. It was time to move on to the town to pick up Kathy. We both had stories for her that would blow her mind as it did ours.

After a few hours, we drove up to Kathy's house. Her husband had heard us coming and was waiting for us at the door. Soon after, Kathy stepped out of the house and told her husband goodbye and that she would be flying back in a couple of weeks. She said she would call him with all the details on when he could pick her up.

Betty and I waved at him, and soon Kathy was in the back seat, reading for what she thought would be a fun vacation. After all of this, I was questioning it, but was certain that once we got to the cabin, we would have plenty to do to have some fun.

Kathy lived closer to the Wyoming border and I knew that within a couple of days—if that, we would be at the place I would call home until I could get a job and find another home to live in.

"Kathy, would you like to hear something really scary?" I asked.

"Sure, Peggy. When we went camping in high school, you always came up with some good ones when we sat around the campfire," she replied.

"Well, the ones that I am going to tell you now aren't made up. They are real, and one happened when I was alone, and the other one happened to both myself and Betty. What I am going to tell you will maybe give you a nightmare, and you can be thankful that you weren't with us to experience it," I replied.

"OMG, Peggy. What happened?" Kathy asked.

"Along the way, I encountered a young girl who was hitchhiking on a quiet highway. It was starting to get late in the day and I didn't want her walking alone, so I stopped to pick her up. She was dressed in a really old dress that looked like something worn dating back to the 1900s. She was very quiet and just kept looking straight ahead as I drove her to the spot where she wanted to get out. She was very pale in color and thin.

"When she got into my car, she was hanging onto a light blue rose. When she left the car, she had forgotten it. I turned the car around and went back to the spot where I had let her off. I didn't see her, so I got out of the car to try to find her before she got too far away. Instead of finding her, I found a graveyard. As I was walking, I came across a tombstone that had a picture on it. It was of the same girl that I had given a ride. I laid the rose down on her grave and before I could walk away, the rose turned black. I ran out of there, jumped in my car and sped away.

"When I stopped, a person told me the story of the walking young girl, who was dead, that walked on that same road every day. For those, I guess, that didn't bother to give her a ride, the myth was that they had bad luck the rest of their lives."

"You've got to be kidding me, Peggy. Okay, you have scared me. That story was a good one," Kathy replied, laughing.

"Laugh, if you want, Kathy, but like I said, it is

very true."

"I've got another true story for you, Kathy, that happened to both Peggy and myself," Betty said.

Without a word, Kathy sat there, listening and hanging on every word that Betty spoke.

"When Peggy and I were driving down the interstate, we had a huge oil truck come barreling up on us. It kept getting closer and closer to the back of the car and wasn't pulling back. Peggy had to go faster, to keep from getting hit. She would change lanes and the oil truck would change lanes behind her. Then, when she went back into the other lane, the truck did the same thing. The loud horn sounded many times, and Peggy was trying hard to stay focused on our safety, the truck and the highway.

"We came to a hill and Peggy floored it, so that we had that advantage to get away from the truck. After we had gotten down off the hill, we thought we were safe and that we had outrun it. When we looked again, we saw the truck coming up behind us, sounding its horn as loud as it could be. We knew that once again we were in danger. Peggy drove faster and faster, knowing that eventually the truck would need to start slowing down as there was a town up ahead. We both kept watching the truck from each side mirror.

"Peggy looked and I looked, and we saw the truck, and then a second later, we both looked and the truck had disappeared. It was nowhere in sight. When we got to the small town, we pulled into a truck stop to report the driver that was trying to kill us. Peggy talked to a state trooper who was there, and told him the story. He told us that this truck runs up and down the interstate all the time, and that they had a lot of people report the same story to him. The truck would be there, and then a second later, it would be gone. He told us that they call it the ghost truck without a driver."

"OMG, Betty! I hope none of these things happen when I am with you, as my heart couldn't take it!"

Kathy had then realized that the stories we had just told her were real, and not scary campfire stories for entertainment.

It was quiet in the car as we traveled down the highway. I knew what Kathy was thinking about and what Betty and I were reliving in our minds.

We came to a motel for the night that also had a café close by. We agreed on no more ghost conversations and went in to eat. \

On the radio, a person was talking about two men that had escaped from a state mental hospital. They were armed and dangerous. They said that they suspected they were hiding out in the mountains somewhere, and wanted everyone to be careful when opening their doors to a stranger.

The exact location was not given, but just another thing to think about.

It wasn't long before we all were asleep. Morning came fast and we were out of there. We had a couple of hours left in driving time before we would reach the cabin. We were relaxed and laughing, in spite of the news report and the current events of the trip.

When I turned off the highway in the direction of the cabin at the end of the road, I was even more excited. I was out of the city and going to a place with clean air and clean water to drink, much different than parts of the city where I had been.

The cabin seemed isolated when we arrived. It was very old and somewhat rundown on the outside, but it would work for me—and us, for now.

There was a pond on the property on a trail behind the cabin, and I was told it had numerous fish in it, for many meals of great-tasting trout. Fishing was on our list of things fun and enjoyable to do for the next couple of weeks. For me, it would be longer as this cabin was my home until I could find another one.

We unloaded the car and walked to the door. I had a key that was furnished to me when I was in the city.

As we entered the cabin and looked around, it seemed nice and very cozy. Everything was in place and was even supplied with cooking utensils and everything else we would need. Our fun day had started. At least we *believed* that it had.

After we checked out the cabin, we took a walk down a trail until we reached a pond. That must be the one that I was told about. We were checking it out when a young man and an older man approached us.

— 3 —

Unknown Neighbors

"Calvin, look what we found," the younger man said.

"I think we have neighbors, Frank," the older man replied.

"I thought my cabin was going to be isolated with no neighbors," I blurted out, wondering why the people I had rented from didn't tell me about these two men.

"We haven't been here long," Calvin said.

For some reason I didn't know if I liked having two men living close to me, especially after Kathy and Betty went home.

"Okay, we will talk to you another time," I said as Betty, Kathy and I started walking down the trail in the direction of the cabin.

The two men just stood there, watching us. Even though I was not fond of the idea of having them living close by, there might come a time when I might need their help, and if so, I thought that maybe I might be able to count on them, if need be.

By the time we got back to the cabin, it was time to eat, talk and go to bed. Another long day for us.

The next morning, Kathy thought it would be fun to cook breakfast outside on an open pit that was built with bricks. She assured us that everything tasted better cooked outside.

We had carried out what we needed when the two men came walking up to us from out of nowhere.

"I see you are going to do your cooking outside while you are here," Calvin said.

"That is the plan for today anyway," I replied.

"Look here, Frank. These women are going to use the old pit to cook breakfast on," Calvin said.

"Would you like to join us for breakfast?" Kathy asked.

"What do you think, Frank? These nice ladies just asked us if we wanted to stay and eat breakfast with them," Calvin said as he laughed.

"Well, I don't know, Calvin. Should we?" Frank said as he also started laughing.

I didn't know about Betty or Kathy, but I was starting to get the chills. Kathy's invitation shouldn't have been followed by laughter.

"Maybe you two should go now. Kathy is just a nice lady and was extending an invitation to you. We really don't have enough food for all three of us and you, too," I said with kind of a sharp tongue, as I didn't find their laughter funny.

"Is the nice lady asking us to leave, Calvin?" Frank asked again with laughter.

"It appears to be that way," Calvin said.

"We will leave, but will be back before long," Frank said.

By the time they were walking away, Betty was done cooking. All of us took everything inside the cabin. I was feeling very uncomfortable about these two men now. I didn't want to scare my friends as they were expecting a good vacation, and not one of fear.

Inside the cabin I asked them what they would like to do for the day. We all agreed that a drive into the small town would be nice. This would give us a chance to see the town and pick up some more food for the time being.

As we drove down the street of the small town, we were amazed at what we saw. There was a small post office on the corner, like none that any of us were accustomed to. A fairgrounds with farm animals in stalls, with people sitting and watching a rodeo. There was a tiny gas station with more people standing around, talking and enjoying the country air and the small town life.

I felt blessed that this area would be my new home for the rest of my life. Kathy and Betty told me that maybe someday they, too, could move here. Our day was full of nothing but sunshine and happiness.

We got some more food and started back up the road to the cabin. When we arrived, we carried everything inside and continued to talk about the difference in city life and country life.

The day passed by quickly, and once again it was time to go to bed. We thought that tomorrow was going to be a wonderful and uneventful day.

In the morning I was up first, standing at the old stove, making coffee for everyone. Today we would be eating breakfast inside.

Soon Kathy and Betty woke up and joined me in the small kitchen. Still wearing night clothes and our robes, we sat there talking about what to do that day. There was so much to explore and do that wasn't that far away from the cabin.

After much deliberation, we decided to take a long walk down the country road, to see everything that we could. We were all excited about another fun day in the country sun.

After getting dressed and ready to walk out the door, once again we saw Calvin and Frank walking up to the door. They were starting to annoy me.

I opened the door and Frank said, "My, my, aren't you up early this morning!"

"Yes we are, and we are getting ready to leave for the day," I replied.

"I came here to borrow some eggs from you."

"Okay, how many do you need?" I asked.

"I don't know. Maybe six or eight will do for the day."

I walked back to the kitchen and got ten eggs out of the fridge, in hopes that this would tide them over for a few days. I felt that they were being too friendly, and none of us wanted or needed that, as we were there to have fun … and no company.

"That will do for the day," Frank said.

"Okay, well, you need to leave now," I replied.

"You are getting pretty good at asking us to leave," Frank said with a small laugh.

"Look, Frank. We are trying to enjoy a vacation, and you and Calvin keep showing up. Would it be too much to ask you to just stay away for a while?"

"I'm not sure that will work," Frank replied.

"What do you mean?" I asked.

"You will see later," Frank said.

Now I was really getting creeped out as I had never had anyone talk to me like that before. The plan was not to answer the door the next time they showed up.

Kathy and Betty agreed that this would be the best idea of the day.

After ample enough time for the two men to leave, Betty, Kathy and I picked up a picnic basket with plenty of food and drink. We were on our way to the unknown wilderness to see whatever we could see.

As we walked down the road, it led us further into

the woods. Along the way, we found wildflowers that we picked and pretty rocks that were lying on the ground. We saw little animals running everywhere and hoped that we didn't see any larger ones, like bears, mountain lions or anything else that might want to eat us for lunch.

We had walked for miles, going and coming back to the cabin. The sun was starting to go down and we needed to get back to a safe place.

When we entered the cabin, Kathy was putting the wildflowers into a vase that she had found under the sink and was filling it with water. Betty had gone to the fridge and was getting ready to start supper for us. It would be burgers and fries that night for supper.

I, on the other hand, was looking for some small screws to fix the deadbolt on the cabin door. I didn't know what to expect now from Calvin and Frank, and wanted to make their entrance harder if we were in there asleep and didn't hear them come through the door.

After we were done with supper and everything else for the day, again we sat and talked about all the fun we were having, with seeing the small pond to fish in, the little town that we all fell in love with, and the walk that we had taken to enjoy all of the nature surrounding us.

After many hours of talking and laughing about all the crazy things we did in high school, it was time to go to bed. I had finished fixing the deadbolt on the door and felt more comfortable with all of us being protected. I was ready for a good night of sleep.

In the morning, when we all woke up, it was another day of discussion on what our plans would be. Betty wanted to go fishing in the pond, and Kathy wanted to go back into town and look through the antique shops. I just wanted to keep away from the strange men that kept showing up at the door.

After a lot of talking, we decided that we could do all three.

Unfortunately, this was another day that didn't happen as well as it should have. There was a knock at the door and apparently the two men were back.

Kathy said that she would answer the door this time and get rid of them.

When she opened the door, she expected the two men to be standing there. Instead, she was met by a man in uniform.

"Good morning, Officer," Kathy said.

"Good morning. I am sorry to bother you, but I'm checking to see if each one of you living or staying around this area have seen any strange men wandering around. Both men escaped from the State Mental Hospital. They are dangerous."

"No, we haven't talked or seen anyone other than a couple of men that live here. They are annoying, but as far as we can tell, are not insane."

"Okay. If you do, stay away from them. When you can, give the Sheriff's office a call and we will know approximately where to look for them," the officer replied.

He walked away and Kathy shut the door, hoping that none of us would see these men that they were looking for.

We got dressed and went to the pond first, to catch fish for breakfast. At least this was our plan. After a couple of hours of no luck and not seeing a fish even jump in the water, we walked back to the cabin.

Meeting us at the cabin door were the two annoying men that kept coming around to antagonize us.

"Why are you here today?" I asked them.

"Did you hear that, Frank? The lady wants to know why we came over here again today," Calvin said.

"I heard all right, Calvin," Frank said with another one of his laughs.

"We came to borrow some eggs from you again," Calvin said.

"I can give you another six or eight eggs, and then that is all I can give," I told him.

"That will last us today," Calvin replied.

"Nice cabin you have here," Frank said as he moved around me to enter the cabin.

After he walked in, Calvin walked in as well. They both stood there, looking at everything and walking around, looking in every room.

"Nice place you have here, ladies," Calvin said.

"What do the two of you think you are doing? We didn't invite you in here. You need to go *now*, and don't come back," I told them with a raised voice.

At that moment, Calvin shut the door and locked it. They weren't going anywhere, and we were trapped inside the cabin.

"I don't think so, missy. We aren't leaving," Calvin replied.

"Why are you doing this to us? We are three women that came here just to have fun and not be held hostage," Betty told them.

"We noticed the cop at your door. He has already been here and he won't be back," Calvin told Betty.

This is when we knew that these two men weren't just annoying, they were the ones that the officer had been looking for. There was no way we could get out of there alive if we wanted to. We had been told that they were dangerous.

"If you leave, we promise not to tell anyone that you were here," I said, trying to trick them into going.

"Check this out, Frank. This little lady wants us to leave, saying that she won't call the cops on us. What do you think about that?" Calvin said, again laughing harder than he had before.

"Ladies, we might be insane, but we aren't stupid," Calvin said.

Kathy decided to make a run for the door. I guess she thought that since she was closer to it, she could do this without Calvin and Frank seeing her. I knew she was doing this out of fear, but there was no way that the two crazy men were going to let her get out that door. The Sheriff and his men were looking for them.

Calvin ran to the door and grabbed Kathy. He had a tight grip on her arms as he held them behind her back. He jerked her around and said, "Don't ever think you can escape from us again!"

Frank then told us to get their breakfast ready and that they liked eggs.

Kathy was so afraid that she could hardly move. Betty and I walked over to her and helped her to the kitchen. We, too, were terrified, but knew that we had no choice but to do what they told us.

Frank turned on the radio, to listen to the news report, to see if there were any new reports in the area about them.

Calvin lit up a cigar and sat in the chair, watching our every move.

When we were in the kitchen, I whispered to Kathy and Betty that they were to do what the men said, while I thought of a way to get us out of here.

They both whispered back that they would do what was asked of them, but were very afraid. They weren't the only ones. I was terrified as well.

When the eggs were done, I took them over to Calvin and Frank. Then I asked them if they would like a cup of coffee to go with it. I had a bottle of sleep medication sitting on a shelf up above the stove that I had brought with me from the city, and thought that if they said yes, I would put some of the pills in their coffee. This would make them sleepy enough to fall asleep, so that we could run out of there.

Calvin was not a stupid man. He was insane, but told me, "You are being very nice to us now, missy. See, the only problem is, that we don't trust you. If we want coffee, we will make our own."

Seeing that this plan wasn't going to happen, I had to come up with another one.

"I know that you don't trust us. You can, though! We are just afraid of you, and if you will let us go, we promise we won't go to the Sheriff. In fact, you can even stay here, where there is plenty of food and other supplies, until it is safe enough for you to move on to another place to be safe," I told Calvin, since he was the oldest of the two men.

"Look, lady, you might think we are dumb because we are insane. We are not stupid enough to fall for that line of bull crap! You are being way too nice, and there is no way that any of you are going to leave this cabin," Calvin replied with a mean look in his eyes.

I knew that this could be a long haul and was not only wondering what was next, but feeling really bad for involving my two best friends in this mess.

On the radio we heard, "We have a report for you from the Sheriff's Office. The two men that escaped from the state mental hospital, that are insane and dangerous, have been spotted in the wooded area of Madison County. At the moment, the Sheriff has brought in extra men to search the area on foot with search and rescue dogs. For those of you that live in the area, close to or in Madison County, the Sheriff's

Department is advising you to bolt your doors and do not leave your home or cabin, for any reason, until you are instructed that the two men have been caught. Remember, this is an emergency message from the Sheriff's Office."

At that moment, Kathy, Betty and I looked at each other. We all could tell that we were in extreme danger and our anxiety was out of control. We also knew that there was a good chance that none of us was going to make it out of there alive.

The day continued with all three of us sitting quietly and not saying a word. We didn't want to make the men mad.

Outside we could hear dogs barking and knew that the search and rescue team working with the Sheriff's Office wasn't far away. Yet *too* far away to hear one of us scream.

As far as I could tell, neither Calvin nor Frank were carrying a gun. If they were, I think that one of them would have showed it to us by now.

The sun was starting to go down and, before long, it would be dark. We were then asked again to go into the kitchen and fix them something to eat. We hadn't eaten all day, but did as we were told.

I wanted to distract Calvin enough so that he would stop watching our every move. If I could do that, I could also slip the pills in their food. As I reached carefully for the top shelf to get the pill bottle, Calvin suspected something and got up from his chair to meet me in the kitchen.

Luckily, I didn't have the pill bottle in my hands.

"What are you doing in here, missy? Don't forget, I am watching every move you make," Calvin said with another mean look on his face.

"I was just getting ready to take you your supper,"

I replied.

At that moment, Calvin saw the bottle of pills on the shelf.

"Oh, look here, Frank. These nice ladies were going to put these pills in our food. What do you think about that?" Calvin said with a slight laugh.

"Oh yeah? Well, let's see, Calvin. Maybe we should give them what for. We can tie them to these chairs and keep them there, since they want to disobey us, and until we are ready to dispose of them!" Frank said with also a crazy look in his eyes.

Calvin took the plates from my hands and set them down on the counter. He then grabbed my arms and held them to my back, shoving me toward the living room area, where we had been sitting in hard-back kitchen chairs the whole day. He tied my hands behind the chair with the cable that he had wrapped around it and in between it, to where there was no way I could free either one of them.

Then he grabbed Kathy and did the same thing to her as Frank was tying Betty's wrists as well to the chair. The only thing we could do now was try to come up with a plan when they went to sleep that included our hands and ankles being tied. We couldn't move. If we tried, the chairs would fall over.

— 4 —

Our Worst Nightmare

As soon as the chairs made any kind of a movement, I knew that either Calvin or Frank would be checking on us, even if they chose to sleep in a bed.

It was getting later in the night, and before long one or both of them would leave the room. Kathy and Betty had dozed off while sitting in their chairs. I had to stay awake, to see what was next. If they were going to kill us, now would be the time they would do it. I still hadn't seen a gun.

I decided to lay my head on my shoulder and pretend to be asleep. I wanted to hear what they had to say as they weren't saying anything.

After about thirty minutes, I heard Frank ask Calvin if he wanted to take the first watch over us, or if he was supposed to. My guess was that Calvin was the brains of the two. Whatever brains they had left, anyway.

Calvin replied that he would take the first watch over us, to make sure that we kept quiet. I don't know how we could scream, as they had put duct tape around our heads, covering our mouths.

Frank went in one of the bedrooms to sleep, whereas Calvin stayed in the living room, drinking coffee and listening to the radio. He wanted to know what every move was by the Sheriff and his men.

I stayed awake, listening, with my eyes shut, to try to figure out how we were going to get out of this awful mess that we were in. Again, we heard the rescue dogs barking outside the cabin. At one point I wanted to think they were getting closer and would be coming in here to rescue us at any time.

Then I realized that it was nothing but wishful thinking.

After a while, along toward morning, Frank came out of the bedroom and told Calvin that he would take the next watch. It wasn't fair. Those two should be the ones tied up in the chairs instead of us.

My thoughts turned to city life again. How I wished now I hadn't left my job and the hustle and bustle of all the traffic. I would be safe right now, and so would my friends.

Frank went into the kitchen to get some coffee and I sat there, wondering if they were going to kill us in the morning or wait until the Sheriff and his men left the area, so they could make their escape. I needed a plan and the *whats* and *ifs* kept getting in the way of my thinking correctly.

Morning came, and Betty, Kathy and Calvin were awake. I was tired, but more afraid, and knew I had to focus on everything they did and try to outsmart them, if I could.

The sound of the men and dogs had gone away, so maybe they would think that they were in the clear to run now, but with that would come disposing of us before they did.

"Do you want some eggs, Calvin?" Frank asked.

"I will, if you cook. You want to throw some bacon in with it?" he asked.

"Sure. How about some steaming hot coffee to go with it?" Frank said as he held up the coffee pot in front of us, laughing as he knew we were hungry and thirsty.

Calvin turned up the radio as another report came over it.

"We are again interrupting normal broadcasting to once more advise all of you listening that there are two men that are very dangerous that escaped from the state mental hospital. We believe them still to be in Madison County. The Sheriff will continue his search until these men are found. Don't leave your home or cabin, for any reason, unless it is a true emergency. Keep all of your doors and windows locked securely and don't answer the door for anyone, unless they have a uniform on. These men could be anywhere. If you have a phone and see them at your door, call the Sheriff's Office immediately."

This all sounded good, but we were the victims and had no hands free to call or no mouths free of duct tape to speak.

I knew that one or both of them would be watching us and our every move. Our chairs were so far apart from each other that we couldn't untie the other one's hands if we wanted to.

I noticed that Frank kept looking at Betty in a very weird way. It was almost like he was starting to want to do more with her than just talk at her face.

This was something that Calvin hadn't noticed yet, and if he did, it was hard telling what he would say or do next. All I could do was hope that this passed with Frank, as Betty would be in more trouble than she was now.

After they ate, they walked around the cabin like they were very nervous. I know they were wondering if the Sheriff or one of his men would bring a search dog to the cabin, to check on us again. That would be the only hope that I could have now.

When Kathy talked to the officer a couple of days ago, I wished she would have mentioned the two men then, but being very kind and good-natured, she just thought that Calvin and Frank were simply annoying, and maybe somewhat lonely men. They didn't *look* like they were killers. At least not at that time.

Frank continued to watch Betty and occasionally he would smile at her. It was like he was infatuated with her face or her body. This could turn out bad. What was he thinking, and what were his plans for her?

Calvin continued to stay close to the radio.

"Calvin, do you think maybe they might have come across the body of that man and his dog near the pond?" Frank asked.

"Not sure, Frank," Calvin said.

"Do you think they will come back here to check on these women again?"

"I can't say," Calvin replied.

"What do we do next?" Frank asked.

"Just stay here until they get tired of searching the area, and then take the car and leave. The Sheriff will just think that the ladies left the cabin. No one will come in here to find their bones." Calvin laughed an evil laugh, and went to the fridge to get something more to eat.

"If we are going to kill them, Calvin, why don't we just do it now? Before we do, I would like some private time with that cute, blond-haired woman before I cut her throat," Frank said.

"There will be plenty of time for that, Frank. We might need one of them to talk nice to the officer, if he comes to the door again, asking questions. If we kill them now, he will see the car and then he will start wondering why no one here is answering the door.

Seeing this, he will bring the dogs to the house. If the one that answers the door talks nicely to the officer, maybe we will let her come with us. We won't harm her," Calvin said.

"Let it be the nice, pretty blond woman, Calvin. I think I really like her," Frank said with a huge grin on his face.

"Settle down, Frank. I told you the plan. Now let's stick to it," Calvin replied in a gruff voice back to Frank.

This is when I knew that I wasn't wrong about the way Frank had been looking at Betty. Once again, all we could do was sit and wait it out.

The day went by with Calvin listening to the radio and me waiting for a knock on the door. Not knowing for sure who would be the lucky one to answer the door, I thought that if it was me, I would probably want one of my friends to make a noise of some sort in here, to draw attention to the two men.

There was something that I didn't know about. Kathy had a tiny pager that she used for work in her back pocket. When she arrived here safely, she was supposed to page her husband, to let him know. Out of all the excitement, she had failed to do this.

It had been days since she had last seen him, and he was very worried as he knew that Kathy wouldn't forget to let him know she was here. I had seen the pager light up, but didn't think much about it.

Her husband knew where she would be, and I was thinking that maybe he might contact the Sheriff, who would come here again to check things out.

Now I felt some comfort, but still not much as none of us knew what Calvin's plan would be from one minute to the next. Right now he wanted to keep us alive a while longer, and an hour from now, we might all three be at their mercy.

It so happened, though, that I was right. Kathy's husband did contact the Sheriff's Office, to ask them to come out here and make sure we were okay. He had heard the news broadcast about the two men and was worried.

As the day progressed, there was a knock at the door. Calvin, with a large knife, cut the cable tied around Kathy's hands. He told her in a very soft voice that she would live if she kept her mouth shut. He also cut the rope from her ankles and removed the tape from her head that was covering her mouth.

Kathy went to the door. When she opened it, she saw an officer standing there.

"Sorry to bother you, but is there a woman by the name of Kathy Gibbs staying here?" he asked.

"Yes, Officer, that is me," Kathy said as she was trying very hard to compose herself, so that our throats wouldn't get cut if she said the wrong thing.

"Your husband called and wants you to get a hold of him very soon. He said he was worried about your safety," the officer replied.

"Oh, well ... Mark knows that I am okay, Officer. He is just a worry-wort," Kathy replied.

"Okay then, sorry to bother you," the officer said.

Kathy shut the door and went back over to sit in the chair. Betty and I knew that Kathy's husband wasn't named Mark and *that* had been her way of letting the officer know that something was wrong.

We knew that when her husband, Jerry, called the Sheriff's Office, he would have been asked his name and a bunch of information before they would follow up on a call. They were too busy looking for these two men to waste their time on a call from a worried husband whose wife failed to call him back.

It wasn't long after Kathy sat back down in the chair that Calvin said, "You did good, missy. Maybe I will keep you for my own."

"You said I could keep the blond woman, Calvin. That isn't fair," Frank said.

"Oh, shut up, Frank! We aren't keeping any of them," Calvin yelled out.

With Calvin and Frank thinking that the officer had left the cabin area and was on his way somewhere else, they didn't know that the officer had walked away to call for back-up and that the cabin was surrounded by him and many more men, waiting to tear the door down and break the windows to enter.

They all heard him scream at Frank, and then the front door came crashing down, with broken glass everywhere as the other men came flying through the windows with guns pointed at Calvin and Frank.

The horrifying terror was over with. Kathy, Betty and I were free! Kathy had been the one with the right plan.

The search was over, and Kathy, Betty and I had had enough fun at the cabin at the end of the road. With everything that had taken place in there, none of us wanted to stay another night.

My idea of wanting to live out the rest of my life in a small town hadn't changed, as I loved the fresh air and the country people. That would still be my plan. The only plan that did change was the location. I couldn't spend my life around or in a small town that had a state mental hospital just miles from there.

Kathy and Betty left to go home, and I loaded up my car with everything I had brought. I locked the cabin door, or should I say ... what was left of it, and walked to my car.

I sat there for a moment, thinking about all the

experiences I had since I left the city.

The walking hitchhiker that turned out to be a ghost. A huge oil tanker truck that also turned out to be a ghost, and two crazy men that could have killed Kathy, Betty and myself.

If it hadn't been for Kathy's worried husband, and the phony name for her to say, we all would be dead right now with the two men getting ready to drive my car away from here.

I started it and didn't even turn my head to look back at the cabin. I just put the car in gear and drove away in the direction of a different small town, in hopes of picking the right one this time.

Other Books by Jana Nolan

THE OLD HENDERSON MINE

MIND POWER

SOUNDS OF FEAR

SECRETS OF SLEEPING INDIAN MOUNTAIN

Visit her Author Web site at
JanaNolan.com